THE NEW, WINDMILL SERIES

General Editors: Anne and Ian Serraillier

155

MANOJ,
JOBY,
GADHVI.
3DC.

STAN BARSTOW

JOBY

HEINEMANN EDUCATIONAL BOOKS
LONDON

Heinemann Educational Books Ltd
22 Bedford Square, London WC1B 3HH

LONDON   EDINBURGH   MELBOURNE   AUCKLAND
HONG KONG   SINGAPORE   KUALA LUMPUR   NEW DELHI
IBADAN   NAIROBI   JOHANNESBURG
PORTSMOUTH (NH)   KINGSTON

ISBN 0 435 12155 3

First published by Michael Joseph Ltd 1964
First published in the New Windmill Series 1971
Reprinted 1972, 1973, 1974, 1975, 1977, 1978,
1980, 1982, 1983 (twice), 1985

Printed and bound in Great Britain by
William Clowes Limited, Beccles and London

For
my mother
and to the memory of
my father,
who are not the mother
and father in this story

1

Joseph Barry Weston – 'Joby' to almost all who knew him – woke that morning conscious that there was something extraordinary about the day and then, in the seconds between sleeping and full wakefulness, remembered that his mother was going into hospital.

He lay with his eyes open looking at the early sunlight flooding through the drawn curtains.

He hadn't worked out quite what was wrong with his mother, and since nobody apparently wanted to tell him he hadn't persisted with his enquiries. Joby was that kind of boy. He knew, though, that she hadn't been well for some time now and it had become almost familiar to him to see her eyes narrowed in a sudden spasm of pain and her hand clutching up beside her breast. Their own doctor, whom she had finally gone to for advice, had sent her to another man at the hospital in Cressley, a specialist, who knew all about these things. He had told her she would have to come into the hospital where he could look after her himself just as soon as there was a bed for her. Since then, in the waiting weeks, the clutching hand had recurred ever more frequently and the narrowed eyes become an almost permanent part of her expression. Always rather tart, Joby's mother became more snappy about the house, losing her temper over little things until Joby's father withdrew into himself more and more and Joby, as ready as possible to make allowances, tried to imagine what it would be like to have tooth-ache all the time, and how short-tempered that would make you.

So his mother would go into hospital for a few days. He was going to stay with his Aunt Daisy till she came back and his father would stay on at home by himself, making his own breakfast and tea and having his dinner out at work. Joby's cousin Mona, who was out of a job at the moment and couldn't be bothered looking very hard for another one, was to come in and make the bed and wash the pots and dust round now and again and his father would give her something for her trouble.

That was the arrangement, and Joby didn't care much for it. Apart from missing his mother (and he was glad she was going away because they would be sure to make her better and send her home more like her old self) he wasn't very fond of his Aunt Daisy because she was even tarter than his mother and very religious as well.

Yet there was in his life now an excitement which seemed strong enough to carry him through every-thing: seven weeks of summer holiday stretched out, vibrant with promise, before him and at the end of it he would not be going back to Tinsley Road Council School but to the grammar school in Cressley. He could relive now, lying lazily in bed, the thrill of knowing he had got his County Minor Scholarship; the

8

tense moments in the assembly hall while Mr Morrison read out the short list of those who had passed and his stomach tightening into knots until his own name came – last of all because of its initial letter. He couldn't get home fast enough at dinner-time and he had run so hard he almost collapsed when he got there, fighting to get the great news past the heaving gasps for breath.

Joby's mother called up from the foot of the stairs.

'Joby, are you awake? Come on down, now; your breakfast's ready.'

Joby got out of bed and drew back the curtains. It was a lovely golden morning and the sun was hot through the glass. The paper-boy stopped his ramshackle bike under the window and hopped off to push the *Daily Herald* through the letter-slot. Joby never read the paper but he knew that this morning's edition would be full of Hitler because he couldn't help noticing the headlines from time to time and his father's constant 'plaint was that there was 'nowt else but 'Itler in t'papers nowadays.' Joby knew little about Hitler except that he was the boss in Germany and the Germans were a warlike people who liked to wear uniforms and march up and down with guns. He couldn't see much wrong with that except we had already had one war with them and they had nearly started another one last year, when everybody was called into the assembly hall at school and given a gas mask each and told they must take the greatest care of it. Joby's was in the bottom of the fixed wardrobe somewhere. He hadn't looked at it for a long time. After some larking about in them when they were first

9

issued everybody had lost interest.

'Joby! Your breakfast's going cold. Come on, now; you know what a busy morning this is. I shan't call you again.'

Joby shouted back in reply and began to get dressed.

No, Snap was the one who knew all about the big men and what was going on in other countries; and what he didn't know he would make up. Snap could talk for hours, if you let him, about Hitler and Mr Chamberlain and Mussolini. It was he who had first taught Joby the jingle all the kids were singing a couple of years back:

'Will you come to Abyssinia
Will you come?
Will you bring your ammunition
And your gun?
Mussolini will be there
Shooting peanuts in the air,
Will you come to Abyssinia
Will you come?'

Snap *said* he'd composed that, but Joby wasn't sure. The trouble with Snap was he didn't always tell the truth. He wasn't a liar, like some Joby knew, but he let his imagination run away with him. Snap had just about the most wonderful imagination of anybody Joby knew and sometimes you had to shut him up to stop his passing off as gospel things he couldn't possibly know about. He wrote stories, Snap did, filling penny exercise books with stuff about cowboys and deep-sea divers and airmen and his uncle's adventures in the Spanish Civil War, and adding them to the

10

big pile in his cupboard at home that his mother was always threatening to clear out into the dustbin.

The funniest thing about Snap, though, was that with all his imagination and the way he could go on writing stories – and the best of them were very good indeed and every bit as exciting as those in the comics – he wasn't particularly bright at schoolwork and he had failed the County Minor. Joby would be leaving him behind when he went to the grammar school and that was the one bit he was sorry about. Snap was Joby's best friend and he liked him a lot, even if some of the other lads, like Gus Wilson, did call him Copperknob and Rednut and make fun of him because he spouted a lot of wild talk and wasn't any good at games.

'JOBY!'

'Co-oming.'

He went down, wading into the torrent of his mother's words and fording it equably.

'I've got to get dressed properly, haven't I? You didn't want me to come down in me pyjamas, did you?'

'We'll have less of your answering back. Get to the table for your breakfast. We've a lot to do this morning.'

She put a couple of sausages and some fried bread on his plate.

'You haven't forgotten what day it is, have you?'

'I know,' Joby said.

'Well, your Auntie Daisy'll be along any minute and I want you to be ready when she gets here. There's your case to pack yet.'

'What case?'

'The case with your shirts and pyjamas and vests. Your Auntie Daisy'll wash your things through but I don't want her to have to come rummaging through the drawers here every time you want a change of underclothes, so I'm sending you off with everything clean for a start.'

Joby's father was sitting on the other side of the table, eating silently and drinking tea from his white pint mug. He had his weekday trousers and waistcoat on but no jacket or tie yet and his shirt-sleeves were rolled back revealing his long, sinewy forearms on which the bold veins criss-crossed like slim, pale-blue snakes.

'Can I take me gun and me bow and arrer?' Joby asked.

His mother, having poured his tea, was already opening drawers in the sideboard and putting clothes into the little attaché case.

'You can't get your bow and arrer into the case so you mun' come back for it one night after your dad's come home from work.'

'I can take me Dinky cars, though, can't I?'

'Not all of 'em. Your Auntie Daisy doesn't want the place cluttering up with all manner of peg-meg. You'd better pick a few out when you've had your breakfast. It's not as though I'm going away for six months.'

'How long will they keep you in?'

'Oh, a few days. It won't be long.'

'Will they let me come and see you?'

'Well, no. They don't let kiddies come because they have to keep the place quiet for them what's really poorly.'

'I know how to be quiet. I can be as quiet as a mouse when I have to be.'

'It's a rule they have. Anyway, I'll be back in no time at all and your dad'll tell you all about it when he's been.'

'I don't know why you wouldn't let your Daisy take you down this morning,' Joby's father grumbled suddenly, ''stead o' me breaking me work an' putting everybody about.'

'Oh aye,' Joby's mother said; 'folk can have mornings off for thick heads and out of idleness, but when you want to take your wife into hospital it's putting people about. Anyway, I told you, it's your place to go then you can get to know all they want you to know, about visiting hours and such.'

'I just don't see any sense in chucking half a day's pay away, that's all. We're not millionaires.'

'No, but you won't have me to keep for a week or two so you'll be that much better off. You know, your trouble is 'at you just don't want to take me in. You'd rather leave it to somebody else.' Joby's father looked sullen.

'I don't like hospitals. They make me go all queer in me insides.'

'You're a big soft lump. It's a pity they're not sticking t'knife into *you*. That'd give you summat to get upset about.'

Joby's head jerked up.

'What knife? Are they going to cut you, Mam?'

'I've got to have an operation, Joby; but it's nothing. They do it every day. I'll be right as rain and home again in no time.'

She straightened up with her back to the window and shadow dimmed the expression on her face at the same time as the sunlight emphasised the lift of her hand. She was wearing her best frock and she smelled like Sunday.

All of a sudden Joby was afraid. He couldn't fathom their adult world, make any sense of it. They talked about a few days to him and weeks to each other. And now, for the first time, he'd learned they were going to cut his mother open. He hadn't realised it was anything as bad as that. For the first time there leaped into his mind the possibility that she wouldn't come back. His mouthful of sausage tasted like a wad of stale bread.

'I don't want you to go,' he said.

He was crying now, helplessly. Grown-ups always seemed so confident, so knowing and sure. Then something like this showed you they were vulnerable too and it knocked the bottom out of everything.

'Don't go, Mam,' he said. 'Don't go.'

She was over by his side, pressing his face into the soft stuff of her frock and stroking his hair.

'There, there. Come on now, Joby. Where's my big brave lad? I've got to go, lad, because if I don't they can't make me better, can they? And the sooner I go the quicker I'll be home again. There's nothing to worry about. Nothing at all. I'll be back again, all done and dusted, before you hardly know I've been away.'

She handed him her own small square of handkerchief.

'Come on, now, dry your eyes before your Auntie

14

Daisy comes. We don't want her to see you've been crying, do we?'

Joby dried his tears and sniffed several times.

'Hurry up and finish your breakfast; that sounds like your Auntie Daisy now,' his mother said as there was a tap on the back door.

But Auntie Daisy would have opened the door and walked in after the first knock, and now the sound was repeated. Joby's mother went into the scullery. There was a murmur of voices and then she came back.

'That young Sidney Prendergast asking if you were in. As if we haven't enough to do without him hanging around.'

'Snap?' Joby jumped up. 'I want to see him.'

He ran out through the back door and along the yard to the street. Snap was slouching along, hands in pockets, some distance away.

'Oy, Snap!'

Snap straightened up and turned round. When he indulged in any definite physical movement he gave the impression that he might come apart at the joints, he was so lanky and loosely built, his legs long, slightly knock-kneed and wayward, like those of a young colt. Freckles crowded his face behind wire-framed glasses and his teeth were big and misshapen in a mouth that was loose and usually laughing. But the most startling thing about him was his cap of tough, violently ginger hair. Once seen, Snap was remembered; and you could see him coming a quarter of a mile away.

Snap retraced his steps a little way, then stopped, scuffing the toe of one shoe in the gutter.

'I can't come out this morning,' Joby said.

'No, your mam said so.'

'She's going into hospital today.'

'Yeh, you told me before.'

'An' I'm gunna stay at me Auntie Daisy's.'

'Yeh, you told me.'

There was a silence.

'I might be able to call for you this afternoon.'

'I shan't be in. I'm going to Leeds with me mam, shopping.'

'Oh.'

'We're gunna have us teas in Lewis's cafe.'

'Oh . . . Happen I'll come down an' call for you tonight, then.'

'I dunno what time we'll be back but you can come down an' see, if you like.'

'Okay . . .'

Snap moved a few steps nearer, trailing his foot along the edge of the kerb.

'Have you been roarin'?'

'No,' Joby said. 'Why?'

'Thought you had.'

'I got summat in me eye.'

'Oh, I see . . .'

Joby saw beyond Snap the figure of his Aunt Daisy as, with her daughter Mona, she turned into the street by the corner off-licence.

'I can see me auntie coming so I'll have to go back in now.'

'Righto,' Snap said.

'I'll see you later, then.'

'Yeh, see you later.'

'If you're not in tonight I'll call for you tomorrow morning.'

'Righto.'

Joby turned.

'So long, then, Snap.'

Snap lifted one hand. 'So long, Joby.'

He mooched off towards the advancing figures of Joby's aunt and cousin and Joby went back into the house.

'Snap,' Joby's mother said. 'Where ever did he pick a name like that up?'

'It's his initials. Sidney, Norman, Arthur Prendergast. S-N-A-P. See?'

'Sidney, Norman, Arthur ... Well, that's a right mouthful, an' no mistake. Nearly comes up to t'Royal Family. I make no wonder he's a bit dozy with a stringful o' names like that hanging round his neck.'

'Snap's not dozy. He's got lots o' brains.'

'He doesn't show much sign of 'em.'

'He thinks a lot an' writes it all down in books.'

'Oh, does he?'

'He says he's gunna get 'em published when he's older. He says he'd send 'em up now, only they wouldn't believe he'd written 'em if they found out he was only eleven, so he's waiting till he's sixteen and he'll send 'em up then.'

'He's got big ideas.'

'He's full of ideas, is Snap. He's got more ideas than anybody else I know.'

'Well you'll meet a lot more boys when you get to the grammar school, so happen you won't want to see so much of him.'

Joby didn't follow the logic of this so he said nothing.

'An' you'd better be getting them Dinky cars sorted out if you're taking any with you. Your Auntie Daisy'll be here any time now.'

'She's coming up the street now with our Mona,' Joby told her.

Joby's father was still at the table, the breakfast pots pushed back and the morning paper spread out before him.

'That bloomin' 'Itler's at it again,' he said. 'Bletherin' about Poland now. He's getting a sight too big for his boots, that feller.'

'Aye,' Joby's mother said dryly, 'I reckon you an' your pal Mr Churchill 'ull have to teach him a lesson.'

'It's about time somebody did,' Joby's father retorted. 'Wes'll have to fight him afore we've finished, or I know nowt about owt.'

'It's time you were getting your collar and tie on,' Joby's mother said.

Weston looked at the clock. 'It's only half-past nine and we haven't to be there till half-past ten.'

'You never know how the buses will be. And anyway, I don't like arriving at last push up.'

'Nip upstairs an' fetch 'em for me, Joby,' his father said. 'They're on t'chest o' drawers. See if you can find a front collar-stud an' all.'

Joby went off on his errand and was just coming down again when Aunt Daisy, having negotiated the long length of Runcible Street, called out at the back door 'Anybody in' and sailed through the scullery with her daughter Mona in silent tow.

Aunt Daisy and Joby's mother were the eldest and youngest respectively of a family of two brothers and two sisters. Of the brothers, one had a small plumbing business in Calderford and the other had emigrated to Australia two years ago. Aunt Daisy had put on weight during her first pregnancy (the baby had died in infancy) and never lost it again. She was out of breath now from her sustained fight with the steady incline of the street and she sat down heavily on a straight chair by the table and took her breath between parted lips.

'About time they run a bus up Runcible Street,' she said, her bosom rising and falling under her shapeless black coat.

'You'll have to get Ted to put a word in at the depot,' Joby's father said. He picked up the collar and tie that Joby had brought for him and stood with bent knees to look into the sideboard mirror.

'Well, you'd no need to trail round, Daisy,' said Joby's mother. 'We could have sent Joby on by himself from the bus stop.'

'Oh, I thought I might be able to give you a hand with summat,' Aunt Daisy said. She was in fact disappointed that, after accompanying Joby's mother on her visit to the specialist, she was not to take her into hospital. 'You're sure you don't want me to come with you this morning?'

'No, thanks all the same, Daisy. But we'll manage.'

'I've been telling her 'at she should ha' let you go with her when you first offered, Daisy,' Joby's father said. 'But she wouldn't have it.'

'Now let's not start that all over again,' Joby's

19

mother said. 'You're taking me and that's the end of it.'

'Aye, I've broken me work now, so we may as well let the arrangement stand.'

A curious change had come over Joby's father's voice with the entry of Aunt Daisy and Mona. From surly and reluctant it had taken on a bantering cheerfulness that showed even more as he spoke to his niece.

'Well, come on, Mona; sit yourself down, lass. It's free.'

'Aye, sit down and don't get under t'feet, Mona,' her mother said.

Mona, who had been standing silently behind the table, moved to a chair.

'Could you drink a cup o' tea, Daisy?' Joby's mother asked. 'There's some left in the pot and it's only been made a few minutes.'

Aunt Daisy said she was always ready for a cup of tea.

'What about you, Mona?'

'I'll have a drink o' pop, if you've got some,' Mona said.

Joby's mother and Aunt Daisy exchanged a quick glance. It seemed to both of them that there was, at twenty-two, something immature and unawakened about Mona, and this preference for 'pop' instead of tea was a small instance of it.

Mona favoured her father in appearance, Joby's Uncle Ted, who was a bus driver for the Calder Valley Transport Company. She was a languid dark-haired girl with a slim waist and big breasts which she had got into the habit of trying to diminish by carrying herself round-shouldered. The rather sullen handsomeness of her face was marred by the slight suggestion of a cast in her left eye. She went through life in a kind of semi-dreamlike state, as though her thoughts were fixed on something totally removed from the world about her. She often did not answer when people spoke to her.

It was this waking dream in which she lived that had caused her to have a dozen or more jobs since leaving school, some in mills but most as assistant in various shops in the town. She had been sacked several times and in the other cases she had left of her own accord, either because of the unsuitability of the work or in the face of the criticism her vagueness brought down upon her from her exasperated employers. Since she was a solitary girl with no close friends and little taste for gadding about or buying new clothes she had managed to save and always had a little money to tide her over between positions.

Joby fetched the remains of a pint bottle of dandelion and burdock from the cellar-head and his mother rinsed out a cup for Mona.

'You don't mind a cup, do you, Mona? I'd get you a glass only I don't want to make any extra washing-up this morning.'

'Never you mind about the washing-up,' Aunt Daisy said. 'Our Mona 'ull see to that for you.'

'An' you know what to do while I'm away, Mona?' Joby's mother said. 'Just pop round in a morning and make your Uncle Reg's bed and wash up any pots he's left. You can run round with a duster as well but there'll be nothing else for you to do. I've had a good clean-down this week.'

Aunt Daisy's glance flickered round the room and if she was looking for something to criticise she found nothing. Apart from the breakfast pots the house was as clean and neat as it always was, the lace curtains freshly hung, the furniture polished and dusted, the low fire burning in a gleaming black-leaded grate.

'Your mam's going to rinse Joby's clothes through, but there won't be any washing for your Uncle Reg because he's sending what he has to the laundry. An' he'll do his own bit o' shopping as he needs to.'

'And have his week-end dinners at our house,' Aunt Daisy added.

Joby, setting out his Dinky cars on the cupboard under the small window, reflected that it more and more sounded as if his mother would be away longer than she pretended to him.

'You know I'd come and do it for you meself, Norah,' Auntie Daisy said. 'Only it's such a pull up that street. An' anyway, our Mona's as well off doing that as hanging about at home.'

'Oh, wes'll manage, shan't we, Mona love?' Joby's father exclaimed in that same curiously bright voice. 'It'll give her a bit o' practice for when she finds a chap. Have you started courting yet?'

'Courting!' Aunt Daisy sniffed. 'I tell her she's too slow to catch a cold, let alone a chap. There's that nice young feller Henry Musgrave three doors up from us. A right steady clean-living young chap. I'm sure he'd be interested if only she'd give him a bit of encouragement.'

'Oh, Mam,' Mona muttered.

'Well, it's about time you were stirring yourself. You can't stop at home for ever.'

'But I don't like Henry Musgrave.'

'An' what's wrong with him, pray?'

'There's nothing wrong with him. He's a nice lad. Only I just don't want to court him, that's all.'

'A bird in the hand's worth two in the bush,' Aunt Daisy said. 'If you're waiting for Prince Charming to ride up on a white horse you'll be at home when you're seventy. And me and your dad won't be here on earth to give you advice then.'

'Oh, shurrup about it, Mam,' Mona said.

'Oh well, advice is fine for them as'll take it. You'll remember your mother's words one day. Happen when it's too late.'

'Oh, she'll start courting all in good time, won't you, Mona?' Joby's father said. 'When Mister Right comes along, eh?'

'Oh aye, you encourage her,' Aunt Daisy said.

Joby, poring over the brightly coloured fleet of Dinky cars, tried to decide which of them he wanted most to take. His eyes lingered on the Rolls Royce Phantom, the S.S. Jaguar, the M.G. Midget, the Hispano Suiza racing car. He had also had a bright yellow open Frazer Nash, the loss of which constituted one of the recent minor tragedies of his life. He had bought it, like the rest, with his Saturday sixpence spending money and running it in the gutter watched it unaccountably gather speed and disappear between the bars of a grate and plunge into the black water below.

'Is t'lad ready?' Aunt Daisy asked.

'All about. He's just sorting a few of his Dinky cars out to take with him.'

Joby began to select, moving cars to one side in a row of special favourites.

'I thought we could all walk down to the bus stop together.'

'Bus,' Aunt Daisy snorted. 'Been me, I'd ha' made Ted get me a taxi.'

Joby's father turned, brush and comb in hand, from the mirror.

'Nah look, she can have a taxi if she wants one. She's only got to say and I'll go down to the corner and ring up now.'

'It's when you get things without asking 'at they mean the most, Reg,' Aunt Daisy told him.

'I can't read women's minds. How do I know when they—'

'It's all right, it's all right,' Joby's mother cut in. 'I never said anything about a taxi because I don't want one. The bus is good enough. I'm not bedridden, after all.'

'No, but you're poorly, Norah. Why else are they taking you in?'

'Aye, I'm poorly, all right. I've been poorly for some time, and carrying on as usual. I don't see why I should start acting like an invalid now.'

'You can have a taxi if you want one,' Joby's father said. 'There's still time to ring up.'

'I don't want one, Reg. I said I didn't want one and I don't . . . Now, for God's sake, let's get cleared up and get off.'

24

2

Joby and Snap dangled their legs from the stone wall at the end of the lane where Snap lived.

'An' this feller 'at came to me Auntie Daisy's chapel said they were setting fire to the churches. You can't say that's right, Snap.'

'No, but the Fashists 'ud filled the churches full of guns an' ammunition, an' that's not right, either, is it?'

'No,' Joby conceded. 'No, that's not right.'

It was, in fact, hard to decide what, or rather who, was right and who was wrong. On the pictures the good and the bad were always clearly defined and the goodies always won. Here in real life, and not so far removed from their own lives since they had a connection with it through Snap's uncle, it was all mixed up and you didn't know where you were.

'An' the Fashists are the mates of the Nazzis in Germany, an' we don't like them, do we?'

'No, we don't. Me dad says wes'll have to fight 'em before we've finished.'

'So does me Uncle Bill. He says we should ha' stood up to 'em years ago when they started their tricks in Abyssinia.'

'Who?'

'The Eyeties.'

'I though we were talking about the Gerries.'

'Well the Eyeties are Fashists, an' all. Them an' the Gerries helped the Fashists in Spain. Rotten dogs, the lot of 'em!'

Snap leaped down off the wall and began to swing at thistles with his stick, capering about in a wild excess of energy and shouting, 'Rotten dogs, dirty swine, stinking pigs.'

Gosh, but it was amazing what a grasp Snap had of world affairs!

'Ey,' Snap said suddenly, standing in a host of beheaded thistles. 'Guess who I saw in Leeds today. Go on, have a guess.'

'Er . . .' Joby had no idea who Snap could have seen so he fell back on facetiousness. 'Gary Cooper.'

'Aw, you're not guessing properly.'

'Well I dunno. Tell us.'

'I'll give you a clue. Female.'

'Er . . . Miss Roper.'

'Naw . . .' Snap groaned in disgust. 'Not old Ropey. I wouldn't tell you if I'd seen her.' He jumped back on to the wall and brandished his stick like a board-pointer and looked along his nose. 'Now, how many of you disgusting little boys have not washed their hands this morning?'

'Ey, I say,' Joby said. 'When Ned Cooke walked out to the front that time with all his shirt lap hanging out at the back.'

They began to giggle.

'An all t'lasses were having fits.'

26

'An' what did old Ropey say? Go on, Snap, you do it best. What did she say?'

Happy in this tribute to his powers of mimicry, Snap looked along his nose again and flourished the stick.

'We can see that your shirt needs washing, Cooke, without you showing us so much of it.'

'Yeh, that was it.'

'And Cookie just stood and looked at her and dropped that terrific fart.'

'Yeh.'

Joby collapsed in laughter. They rolled and squirmed together on top of the wall until they had extracted all they could from the memory. Then Snap said:

'You haven't guessed who I saw yet.'

Joby had lost interest. 'I can't guess.'

'You can if you try.'

'I can't be bothered.'

'I won't tell, then.'

'Okay. I don't care.'

Snap gave a sideways look at Joby.

'You would if you knew who it was.'

'Well if you won't tell me I won't know, so it doesn't matter.'

That had him, Joby thought. He lay on his back on top of the wall and waited for Snap to make the next move. Of course, he was absolutely bursting to tell . . .

'I'll give you another clue,' Snap said. 'She's some- body special.'

'Well, if she wasn't somebody special you wouldn't be making all this fuss about her, would you?'

'She's somebody special to you. Somebody you like a right lot.'

The light came on in Joby's mind. He knew now who it was but he couldn't say because that would be to acknowledge the accuracy of Snap's description.

'Mae West.'

'Aw, you're acting again.'

Joby sat up and slid off the wall. 'Come on, let's buzz off somewhere else.'

'I'll give you another clue,' Snap said. 'That's three. She wasn't born in England.'

'Mae West,' Joby said again.

'You're kiddin' on purpose,' Snap said. He began to grin, showing his big crooked teeth. 'You've guessed an' you won't let on.'

'How have I guessed?'

'I can tell. You're blushin'. You know who it is because you're blushin'.'

'I tell you I don't know,' Joby shouted. 'An' I don't care. An' if you don't stop actin' about with your guessin' I'm off home.'

'Her initials are E.L.'

'Elsie Lee, then.'

Snap's jaw dropped. 'Who's Elsie Lee?'

'One o' me aunties.'

'I didn't know you had an auntie Elsie.'

'Well, you don't know everything.'

'You haven't got an auntie Elsie.'

'How do you know? I've just said I have, haven't I?'

'I don't believe you.'

'Well, *I* don't care.' Joby turned his back and strolled away. 'Come on, let's go somewhere else.'

Snap came off the wall and fell in beside him.

'Where we going?'

'I dunno.'

'Have we time to go down t'Pastures?'

'I dunno. Mebbe it's too far. Me Auntie Daisy says I've to be in by nine.'

'It must be nearly that now . . . Have I to tell you who it was?'

'You can if you want. I'm not bothered.'

There was a silence, then Joby relented.

'Okay, tell us, then.'

He still had Snap where he wanted him because now it would look as though *he* thought there was something special about the person concerned.

Snap said nothing. Joby softened further.

'Was it Elsa Laedeker?'

Snap brightened. 'You knew all along, didn't you?'

'I guessed just now.'

'Ah, you knew all along. I knew you did.'

'I just thought about the initials and guessed.'

'You knew before that.'

Joby was furious now at the soft way he had delivered himself back into Snap's hands. And angry with Snap because he was taking advantage of his weakness.

He walked faster, kicking at loose stones lying in the lane.

'Wait on,' Snap said.

Joby ignored him.

Snap caught him up. 'Wait on, Joby. Where you going?'

Joby said nothing.

'Don't get mad, Joby,' Snap said. He put his arm across Joby's shoulder and Joby shrugged impatiently under its weight.

'Come on, Joby. Don't get mad.'

'I'm not mad.'

'Y'are. I can see y'are.'

'Is'll get mad if you keep on saying I'm mad.'

'Okay, you're not mad.'

'What if I am mad, anyway? What's it to do with you?'

'I don't want you to be mad with me. We're mates, aren't we?'

Well you could get mad easily with Snap, but you couldn't stay mad with him for long. Joby reached up and took Snap's hand, pulling Snap's arm round his shoulders.

'Okay, we're mates.'

There was a wonderful warmth in the heart when you were with somebody like this. When you had a little quarrel and made it up – really made it up without any resentment left over – it was a time when almost everything was right with you and what wasn't right would be before very long. Joby could almost even visualise Elsa Laedeker smiling at him and stopping to talk to him for a moment, though what he would say to her if she did he couldn't imagine. Stretching it further, he could see her with him in the tuppenny rush at the pictures on a Saturday afternoon, sitting close to him in the semi-darkness and dipping into his bag of mint humbugs while they watched the adventures of Hopalong Cassidy, Johnny Mack Brown and Flash Gordon (in twelve instalments).

And that *was* stretching it, because he'd never seen Elsa at a matinée though he'd once caught sight of her going into the first house in the evening with her father and mother. He supposed that fee-paying students of the prep. department of Cressley Academy drew the line at tuppenny rushes. Which was a pity.

Elsa's father and mother had brought Elsa with them from Germany some years ago. They lived in a big semi-detached house in Park Road, an unmade street with iron posts that stopped anybody driving a car all the way through. Elsa's father had something to do with the wool trade and it must be a good job because Park Road was a pretty posh district where lots of people, including Mr Laedeker, had motor cars. Snap's father said the Laedekers were Jews, and trust the Jews to do all right for themselves. Snap had reported this to Joby and also his uncle Bill getting mad and telling Snap's father he ought to go and join his pal Hitler and see what *he* was doing with the Jews.

Snap's father said everybody was busy calling Hitler names but look how he'd put Germany back on its feet. We could do with a bloke like him in England to shake things up a bit.

Then Snap's uncle said he was talking like a half-wit: he'd no bloody idea at all. We needed a shake-up all right but not one to put a maniac like Hitler on top, giving thugs uniforms and letting them go about dragging people out of their beds and kicking them to death in the streets.

Kicking who to death? Snap's father wanted to know.

The Jews, Snap's uncle told him.

Oh, the Jews, Snap's father said. It's about time that lot were put in their place.

'That started a real row,' Snap said. 'Me uncle Bill

said he wouldn't stop in the house a minute longer and me dad told him he was welcome to clear off any time if he wasn't satisfied.'

'He didn't go, though, did he?' Joby said.

'No; me mother came in and quietened them down.'

Uncle Bill was Snap's mother's brother and he'd lived at Snap's since he came home from Spain. His father and his uncle Bill didn't row all the time but there was always an argument when they got on to world affairs.

'But what *are* the Jews?' Joby said. 'That's what I'd like to know.'

'They're the people who crucified Jesus Christ,' Snap said.

'Oh, I know that,' Joby said. 'But that was ages ago.'

'Well that's what they did and God drove them out of their country as punishment and made them wander all over the world.'

'And now they haven't a country?'

'No. They live all over the world in other people's countries. But they still have a lot of their own rules, like going to the synagogue instead of church, and not eating meat on Fridays.'

'No, that's the Catholics,' Joby said, correcting Snap for once. 'The Macleods down our street are Catholics.'

'Well, the Jews circumcise all their baby boys when they're born.'

'I'm circumcised,' Joby said, 'and I'm not a Jew.'

'It's funny.'

'I don't get it,' Joby said.

'Neither do I,' Snap admitted.

And that in itself was something.

'Well, are we going down t'Pastures?' Snap wanted to know. 'Or are you going home?'

'I dunno what time it is,' Joby said.

It was a lovely warm evening, still broad daylight, and surely too early for him to go back to his Aunt Daisy's and get ready for bed. On the other hand, he didn't want to get his auntie's back up when he didn't know how long he would have to stay with her.

'Well, what say we walk down that way and if we see a feller we'll ask him?'

'Righto,' Joby said.

They wandered off down the lane by the cricket field. Between the lane and the open playing field was a narrow border of trees and unkempt elderberry bushes. They had climbed at least part of the way up most of the trees and carried out numerous death-or-glory cavalry charges across the edge of the cricket pitch. On the far side of the field the evening sun dazzled the windows of Manor Lodge, a large stone house which had been private property many years ago but was now a Working Men's Club. If you narrowed your eyes against the distance it was possible to discern the old men sitting out on the terrace over their peaceful pipes and pints while their younger brethren stooped to the pampered turf of the bowling green inside the thick, close-cropped privet hedge. The lodge had been sited well and sitting on that terrace you looked south-west across the wide valley of the Calder. There was industry enough to east and west but here the chimneys in sight could be counted on one hand,

and an occasional smouldering pit-heap was all that broke the green sweep of the far hills that rolled away to the Pennines.

Below the cricket field the township had over-flowed into a meadow that was three-quarters full of new red-brick council houses. Joby and Snap skirted the estate by keeping to the old hard-trodden field-path and emerged into a wide unsurfaced lane that led by a bridge over the deep cutting which carried the railway line to Blackpool via Trafalgar Street station, Cressley.

There were several boys of their own age on the bridge, some scuffing about in the dust of the lane and two sitting up on the stone parapet over a thirty-foot drop.

'It's Gus Wilson and his lot,' Joby said.

They stopped at the corner of the lane.

'They would be down here,' Snap said. He didn't like Gus because Gus wouldn't leave him alone. Not that anybody really did like Gus, but he always had a gang to boss.

'What d'you wanna do?' Joby asked.

'Well, it's getting late anyway,' Snap said. 'And you've got to be in early.'

'Aye, but they've seen us now,' Joby said. 'They'll think we're running away or summat if we turn back.'

'All right, then,' Snap said. 'I'm not scared of Gus Wilson.'

'Well, neither am I,' Joby said, prepared to stretch the truth a little if Snap was.

'Come on, then.'

'Okay' They strolled with every appearance of non-chalance towards the bridge and Gus Wilson watched

34

them from his position on the parapet, tapping the iron plates with the stick he was swinging between his legs. They knew everybody there but greetings were exchanged with Gus.

'How do, Gus.'

'Now then, Joby. Where you off to?'

'Oh, nowhere. Where you going?'

'Same place. I see you've got Copperknob with you. Ey, Copperknob, made any good lies up lately?'

'What's up with you?' Snap said.

'Nowt. What's up with you?'

'Nowt,' Snap muttered scraping in the dust with his stick.

'Has your uncle shot any more 'planes down lately?' Gus said.

'I never said he had shot any 'planes down,' Snap said.

'Garn, you did. You said he'd shot three 'planes down in Spain.'

'I never did say that.'

'Are you calling me a liar, Gingernut?'

'You're calling me one.'

'That's different.'

'What you been doing, then?' Joby said to divert Gus from Snap.

'Aw, just hanging about. We've been watching a couple in that field. They've got no clothes on.'

'Where?' Joby said. 'Which field?'

'Over there,' Gus pointed with his stick. 'If you stand up here you can see them.'

'Garn, you're kidding.'

'I'm telling you.'

35

Joby looked up at Gus.

'Ah, you'll wait till I'm up there then push me.'

'Think I'm daft enough to push you with a drop like that?'

'Well, I don't believe you, anyway.'

'It's right, In't it, lads?'

'Yeh, it's right, Joby.'

Joby said, 'Okay, I'll have a look.'

He scrambled up on to the parapet and crouched there for a minute. When he stood up he would have his back to Gus and he didn't like that. Nor did he like heights when he had nothing to hang on to. He had climbed across the outside of the river bridge a number of times but there you had grips for both hands and feet ... He lifted himself up and stood upright. His legs felt insubstantial. He told himself not to look down to his right and directed his gaze into the meadow.

'Can't you see 'em?' Gus asked.

'No, I can't.'

'Sure you're looking in the right place?'

'I'm looking all over,' Joby said. 'I can't see owt.'

One of the gang snorted with laughter and Joby wondered what Gus was up to behind him. He daren't look quickly round, though, or he would overbalance.

'C'mon, Gus,' he said. 'Stop kidding.'

'Stand on your toes,' Gus said, 'then you'll see better.'

Joby forced himself up on to his toes. He'd have to get down in a minute.

'Can't you see 'em now?' Gus said. 'Down in that far corner.'

'You're having me on.'

'No, I'm not. There's a couple without clothes on. One of 'em said "moo" when we come past.'

'Ah, cows,' Joby said in disgust. But he was thankful for the excuse to get down off the parapet.

Gus and the gang were all laughing.

'Ever been had,' Gus said. 'Ever been had.'

'Very funny,' Joby said, his feet in the lane again.

'Why aren't you laughing, Copperknob?' Gus said.

'Because I don't feel like it,' Snap said.

'Aw, you don't feel like it, eh?'

'Lay off him, Gus,' Joby said.

'I'm not doing owt to him, am I?'

'No, but lay off. He's all right. He's my mate.'

'You can have him,' Gus said.

It was evident that Gus was in an amiable mood. There were times when he worked up an exchange like that into a quarrel for the fun of it, or to prove something to somebody. But Joby had rarely had anything like real trouble with Gus. He sensed that there was something about him that kept Gus from pushing too far. It couldn't be that Gus was scared of him. He wasn't all that good with his fists and if it came to a straight fight with Gus he thought he would lose, or at least take a terrific hammering in forcing a draw. No, it was that somehow Gus seemed to respect him. Perhaps Gus just liked him. He didn't know. He couldn't think why.

A man came on to the bridge: shortish, bandy legs in brown corduroys. He wore a greasy cap and had a white silk scarf pulled tight round his neck, the ends held down under a navy-blue waistcoat. He chewed a sprig of hawthorn and loped along with a polished thorn stick a pace in front of a dusky greyhound with prominent staring eyes.

'Ey, can you tell us what time it is, mister, please?' Joby called, and the man answered over his shoulder:

'Time you lot were in home.'

Joby turned away, pulling a face, and Snap followed the man ten yards along the lane, walking in an exaggerated imitation of the loping gait that made even Gus and his crowd laugh.

'D'you know what time it is, Gus?' Joby asked.

'Oh, it's early yet. What's up, you haven't to be in, have you?'

'I'm stopping at me Auntie Daisy's. She said I'd to be in by nine.'

'Ah, well, it struck nine long since.'

'It never did.'

'Did, I tell you. I heard the church clock.'

'You can't hear the church clock strike right down here.'

'Oh, well, if you don't want to believe me . . .'

'Happen I'd better push off anyway. You coming, Snap?'

'What you stopping at your auntie's for anyway?' Gus said.

'Me mam's gone into hospital.'

'Is she having a kid?'

'Naw.'

'What's up with her then?'

'I dunno. She's got to have an operation.'

'Are they gunna cut her leg off?'

'Naw, nowt like that.'

'How d'you know if you don't know what's up with her?'

'Well, I know it's not her leg.'

He knew it was something to do with his mother's breast but he couldn't say so for he had no means of description except a word he couldn't use in reference to his mother.

'An auntie of mine went in an' they cut one of her tits off,' Gus said. 'She wears a balloon under her frock on one side now so's it won't show.'

Joby felt his cheeks burn red. He turned away from Gus and his pals and began to walk off.

'So long, then, Gus.'

There was a chorus of so-longs from the gang.

'What you blushin' for?' Snap said when they were some way off.

'I'm not blushing,' Joby said.

'Y'are. You're as red as fire.'

Joby's pulse was agitated. He was scared about what they were going to do to his mother in hospital.

'I'm just hot, that's all,' he said.

Snap was at his most tactlessly persistent.

'Was it what Gus said about his auntie?'

'I'm not blushing,' Joby said angrily. 'Why don't you shurrup saying I'm blushing?'

'Okay,' Snap said after a pause. He shrugged.

They walked on in silence, Snap at the ditch side, swinging at nettles with his stick. At the corner of the cricket field, where Joby could leave Snap and take a short cut to his aunt's house, they stopped and Snap went on slashing with his stick while studiously avoiding looking at Joby.

Joby knew that Snap's feelings were hurt.

'I'll see you tomorrow,' he said.

'Aye, righto.'

'Have I to come down in the morning?'

'If you like.'

'Have we to go down to Gibbert's Dyke and see'f we can catch some newts?'

'If you want to.'

Joby hesitated.

He said, 'If I tell you summat, Snap, will you promise not to tell anybody else?'

'I can keep a secret,' Snap muttered.

'Cross your heart?'

'Cross me heart.'

'That what Gus was talking about . . . about his auntie. Well, I think that's what they're going to do to me mam.'

'I guessed it was,' Snap said.

Joby felt let down.

'How did you guess?'

'Oh, I just guessed.'

'It's still a secret, though.'

'Yeh,' Snap said. 'Okay.'

They said so long and Joby went off up the lane. He hadn't gone far when it struck him that they might already have operated on his mother, and he broke into a fast trot which got him to his Aunt Daisy's at twenty-five to ten. His auntie was cross with him for being late. Mona was sitting on the couch with her legs curled up, reading a comic with a drawing of a nurse in a white uniform on the front. Aunt Daisy had been to the hospital with Joby's father. She said

Joby's mother was having a nice rest in bed and they were going to operate on her the day after tomorrow and he wasn't to worry because everything was going to be all right.

3

The Fashists had gone to ground behind the banking in the field on the far side of the playground. They maintained a sporadic fire from behind their cover and there was an occasional tinkle of breaking glass as another window pane shattered in the bullet-scarred south wing of the school. Joby and his fellow defenders relaxed below the level of the windows, resting after cutting down repeated enemy assaults across the open stretch of tarmac. Elsa sat on the floor beside Joby, tired from the continuous loading and reloading of the rifles which had burned hot in Joby's hands. Joby smiled at her and touched her hand reassuringly.

'Don't worry: there'll be help coming soon.'

The relief column was on its way from Pontefract Barracks. Mr Morrison had got a message through before the telephone lines were cut.

'I'm not afraid,' Elsa told him. 'Not with you here. I think you're so brave, Joby.'

Joby shrugged. 'I'm only doing my duty.'

She gave him a smile that melted his heart as the headmaster came crawling on his hands and knees along the line of defenders.

'Everything all right?' he was asking at intervals. 'Don't worry, help is on its way. We shan't have to hold out much longer.'

'Everything all right here?' he said as he reached Joby and Elsa.

'All in order, sir,' Joby answered.

'Good, good. You're all doing a magnificent job.' Mr Morrison raised his head carefully so that he could see out. 'Well, we seem to have given them something they won't forget in a hurry. I doubt if they'll try another assault now.' He stopped and stared. 'Good lord, look!'

Joby lifted himself up, rifle at the ready. A soldier had clambered over the rim of the banking and was now breaking into a run across the open playground, coming towards the school with a small round object in his right hand.

'It's a hand grenade!' the headmaster cried, and Joby said calmly:

'Leave him to me, sir.'

He had the soldier in his sights already, the rifle barrel resting on the window-ledge and turning slightly as it followed the running figure. He waited deliberately until the soldier halted, drew the pin from the grenade and swung back his arm to throw. Then Joby shot him, the impact of the bullet spinning the man off his feet as the grenade exploded and blew shattered lumps of tarmac into the air.

'Good shot, Joby!' the headmaster cried and Joby, his rifle covering the edge of the field for signs of further movement, said briefly:

'It was nothing, sir.'

Elsa's eyes were turned up to him, glowing with admiration.

He became aware that somebody was talking to him.

'What?' He looked at the dark-smocked barber standing over him.

'I said, do you want your hair cutting or are you just going to sit there all morning?'

Joby said, 'Oh, sorry,' and got up and walked across to the empty chair.

'You were miles away just then, weren't you?' Mr Manley, the barber, said as he shook out the sheet, swung it round Joby in a practised sweep and tucked the edge into his collar.

'I was was just thinking about something.'

'Aye, I could see that. I spoke to you twice afore you answered me.' He was a very tall thin man with a wall eye. He bent now over Joby like a willow wand and clicked his scissors. 'What d'you want, then? A tuppenny all-off?'

Joby smiled at him in the mirror, which was directly opposite the one on the back wall and showed you yourself several times over, getting smaller in the distance.

'A short back and sides, please; but let the fringe alone because I'm training it to go back.'

'Ah, well, in that case wes'll have to make you a parting an' give it a drop o' cream.'

Joby looked at the confusion of bottles, jars and sprays standing between the mirrors as the barber set to work on his hair. Besides stocking several well-known brands, such as Brylcreem, Nufix and Julysia, Mr Manley made his own haircream in the back room

44

and filled it into washed-out medicine bottles and labelled it Pomona Fixative. It was cheap and very popular with young men and boys because it rendered the most unruly hair manageable. Its only fault was that it dried and set shortly after application, transforming the surface of the hair into a thin brittle shell which combed out in a dry powder, like heavy dandruff.

'How's your mam, then?' the barber asked as he switched off the buzzing trimmer and flashed his scissors once more.

'She's in hospital,' Joby said.

'Aye, I heard so.'

The barber's shops were clearing-houses for the town's gossip. Some old men – like the one resting placidly in the corner now, stick between his legs, horny fingers holding his blackened, burnt-down pipe in his unsteady jaw – sat for hours on end, picking up and passing on tit-bits of information, indulging in long rambling arguments about filiation and ancestry, resurrecting long-ago scandals and keeping their ears cocked for new ones. And all this without apparently taking much interest in anything but the slow rumination of whatever was in their minds.

'Has she had her operation yet?' the barber asked Joby.

'Yeh, day before yesterday.'

'Ah well, you might be having her home soon, then?'

'I hope so.'

'Aye, you'll be missing her, I reckon.'

'I'm stopping with me Auntie Daisy,' Joby said.

45

'Oh aye? And what's your dad doing, looking after himself?'

'Me cousin Mona comes round to tidy up for him.'

'I see.'

But the barber-shop talk these days was dominated by one big theme: the threat of war. It had been narrowly averted a year ago but now it looked as though Hitler's appetite was insatiable. The customers were divided. Some believed in Mr Chamberlain's policy of appeasement; others who had called Mr Churchill a warmonger not long ago had come round to the view that he and Mr Eden were right – that we should have already re-armed and made it clear to Germany that there was a line beyond which they wouldn't be allowed to go without war. Now Hitler was sabre-rattling over Poland and it appeared we had a treaty with the Poles. Did Hitler realise we should go to war if Poland was attacked? Would we, in fact, do so? And if it came to that, some of the men in the shop wanted to know, why should we? What had Poland to do with us? Some of them didn't even seem to know where it was.

The talk swung backwards and forwards from one side of the shop to another, reinforced by quotations read aloud from the *Yorkshire Post* and the *Daily Express,* which Mr Manley had delivered to the shop every morning. Under it all, as the barber snipped at his hair, stopping occasionally to make a point and emphasise it with a wave of the long slim scissors, Joby drifted back into day-dreams of Elsa. It was seeing her shopping with her mother in Co-operative Street that had started him off. He had followed them for some time, stopping to look in windows when they did.

Once Mrs Laedeker went into a newsagent's, leaving Elsa gazing into the window on her own. Joby was no more than a dozen feet from her and he watched her covertly, wondering how he could speak to her. But what was the use? She didn't even know him. Her glance, turned his way for a moment, slid over him with neither recognition nor interest. He walked past her, his clothes brushing hers for a second, and took up a similar position on the other side of her. Then her mother came out of the shop and led her away up the hill . . .

The Siege of Tinsley Road School ended with the arrival of the relief column, a company of the King's Own Yorkshire Light Infantry in trucks led by an armoured car. A detachment was sent in pursuit of the Fashists, who were retreating in confusion across the fields, and the commanding officer led the rest of his men into the playground as the defenders ran cheering out of the school. *Some* of them ran. Joby, who had been wounded now, walked out with a blood-stained bandage round his head, one arm in a sling and the other round the shoulders of Elsa, who was supporting her hero.

'He's at it again,' the barber said.

'What?' Joby said.

'Daydreaming. Miles away again. I said do you want it from the bottle or the spray?'

'Er – the spray, please,' Joby said.

'Right you are!'

The barber sprayed Joby's hair liberally and slicked it into place before trimming off one or two stray ends with a last snip-snip of the scissors.

'There,' he said, standing back. 'Your girl friend'll hardly know you now.'

He was joking, of course. Joby tried not to blush as he paid the barber and left the shop.

'Tell your dad I hope your mam'll soon be up and about again,' Mr Manley called after him.

Joby walked down the street feeling rather conspicuous at being so well groomed. He fingered his hair gingerly. Mr Manley had put on a lot of cream and it should stay in place all day if he didn't comb it.

He made his way towards home. It was Friday morning and if Mona was still there he could collect his comic which should have come with the morning paper. There was a comic for almost every day of the week and Joby got two of them: *Wizard* on Tuesday and *Hotspur* on Friday. The others were *Adventure* on Monday, *Rover* on Thursday and *Skipper* on Saturday. They all ran similar kinds of stories but *Hotspur* was Joby's favourite because it featured the exploits of the pupils of Red Circle School. It was possible by swapping to read them all, and *Boy's Cinema* and *Film Fun* as well; but Joby's mother didn't approve of swaps. She had once found a blackclock which she swore had come into the house in a comic. He wished now he had thought to ask Mona to bring the comic up with her because if she had already left he would have to trail all the way back down for it later.

Agnes Macleod was sitting on the wall at the end of the street with three or four boys round her. Agnes had just left school but apparently hadn't started working yet. She was always in the street with big lads round her, either bunching together in a group or circling round and round on bikes. What any of them got out of this Joby didn't know; but they were at it all the time. Mollie, Agnes's younger sister, a year older than Joby, was playing by herself a little farther on. She spoke to Joby as he passed her.

'Hello, Joby.'

'Hello.

'Has your mam come home from hospital yet?'

'No, not yet.'

'Where you stopping while she's away?'

'At me Auntie Daisy's.'

'Oh . . . You're going to grammar school after the holidays, aren't you?'

'Yeh,'

'Are you glad?'

'Yeh; I want to go.'

'I don't like school,' Mollie said. 'I want to leave as soon as I can and get a job like our kid.'

'Has she got a job?'

'Yeh, at Hanson's. She starts on Monday.'

'Well, I've got to go now,' Joby said.

'Righto.'

'Be seeing you.'

'Yeh, so long, Joby. Hope your mam's home soon.'

'Yeh. Thanks.'

Joby wasn't too sure of Mollie. She was a cocky, knowing little piece with bright mocking eyes. You were never sure what she might say next.

The door of the house was unlocked but there was no sign of Mona. He went into the living-room, which was all cleaned up and tidy, and found his comic inside the folds of the *Daily Herald*. He opened it and glanced through the pages, putting off the temptation to start reading it properly. A faint murmur of voices came to his ears. It seemed to be coming from upstairs. He went to the foot of the stairs and looked up. The bedroom doors, opposite each other on the tiny landing, were closed. He called out and after a few seconds the door of the big bedroom opened and Mona came out.

'What're you doing here, Joby?'

'I came to fetch me comic.'

She started to descend towards him, one hand lifted and touching her hair as though she were concerned about its tidiness.

'Have you been cleaning up upstairs?'

'I was talking to your dad. He didn't go to work this morning. He wasn't feeling so well.'

She brushed past without looking at him and he followed her into the living-room.

'Is he in bed?'

'Yes, but he says he'll get up afore long.'

Joby noticed that Mona's cheeks were rather red and she talked as if she were a little out of breath. He supposed she'd been bending down sweeping under the bed, or something.

'What's wrong with me dad?' he said.

'He says it's his stomach 'at's upset. I didn't know what he was gunna do for his dinner; whether he wanted me to run out for some fish and chips for him, or what.'

'Me Auntie Daisy's given me some money to get some fish and chips for us.'

'Yes, well your dad says he can manage.'

'Oh, righto. I think I'll just go and see him before I go.'

'I'll wait and walk up with you, if you like,' Mona said. 'I've done here for today.'

Joby went upstairs and into the big bedroom. His father was lying down under the clothes with only his face showing. Joby stood and looked at him.

'Our Mona says you're feeling poorly.'

'Oh, it's all right, Joby. Me insides are a bit upset, that's all. I'm getting up afore long.'

'I came round to get me comic.'

'You've had your hair cut, I see.'

'Yeh, me Auntie Daisy made me go. Mr Manley was asking about me mam.'

'Is your Auntie Daisy looking after you all right?'

'Yeh, all right. I'd rather be at home, though.'

'I expect you would. Never mind; it won't be long now.'

'Will me mam be coming home soon?'

'As soon as she gets over her operation.'

'When will that be?'

'Not long. They'll just have to keep an eye on her for a bit.'

'Is she still poorly?'

'She'll be better when she comes home. The doctors are very pleased with her.'

'D'you want me to bring the paper up for you?'

'No. I'm getting up in a minute.'

'I'll be going, then. I've got to call for some fish and chips.'

'Aye, all right.'

Joby turned to the door and his father called him back.

'I say . . . I think it might be better if you didn't say owt to your auntie about me being off work. You know what a fussy body she is. She might think she ought to come round.'

'All right,' Joby said. It was reasonable.

'Will you tell our Mona?'

'Righto.'

'An' if you look on top of the drawers there you'll find some change. Take a bob for your spend.'

'Ooh, ta!'

This was a bonus because as far as Joby knew his mother had left some money with Auntie Daisy and his weekly allowance was to come out of this.

Mona was ready when he went downstairs and they walked along the street together.

'Hasn't that lass got owt better to do?' Mona said when they had passed Agnes Macleod and her friends.

'She's allus got lads round her,' Joby said.

'I dare say she'll wind up married afore she's eighteen. Lasses like that usually do.'

'Aren't you gunna get married, then, Mona?' Joby said.

'Happen so,' Mona said. 'When I'm ready.'

There was a silence.

Mona said. 'Does your dad suffer with his stomach a lot?'

It was funny, because Joby couldn't remember it happening before.

'Happen it was summat he ate,' he said.

'Mmm.'

'Oh,' said Joby, remembering, 'he said not to mention it to me Auntie Daisy in case she came round.'

When he glanced at Mona he saw a faint flush of colour in her cheeks. Perhaps she didn't like to tell fibs.

'If you want to tell her I suppose it'll be all right,' he said.

'No, I dare say your dad's right. Me mam is a bit of a fusspot. As long as you don't go an' blurt it out later an' make it worse.'

'Eh?' Joby said.

'Well, if she finds out later she'll be cross at us for keeping it from her.'

'Oh, I shan't say owt.' Joby assured her.

What a lot of bother about nothing, though! He didn't know why they couldn't mention it to Auntie Daisy and let her do as she liked about it. Still, he'd agreed now . . .

He left Mona outside the fish and chip shop and went in alone. Dawson's made the best fish and chips in town, though some people said Naylor's were as good. They were open every night except Wednesday and Sunday, and on two dinner-times as well. The shop was full. Mrs Dawson served while Mr Dawson did the cooking. Every now and then there would be a huge hiss from the fat as Mr Dawson threw another bucket of chips into the pan, and steam clouded the mirrors over the range. Mrs Dawson served expertly, measuring the portions with a practised eye and wrapping them swiftly; but there were ten customers before Joby and two of them were girls in overalls from the mill up the road and they would want at least a dozen parcels each.

Joby settled himself for a wait, leaning against the wall by the door and opening his comic. He felt his stomach start to rumble. He was ready for his dinner. Bought fish and chips and the *Hotspur* made Friday dinner-time one of Joby's favourite times of the week.

4

'Get them knees scrubbed, Joby. Get 'em properly clean.'

Joby was sitting up next to the sink in which there was a bowlful of cooling greyish soapy water.

'By the livin' . . .' Aunt Daisy looked at Joby's legs. 'I've never seen so much muck. I could grow a stone o' taties in it, I'm sure.'

Joby rubbed sullenly at his knees with the flannel. He had no trousers on and though his shirt was tucked down between his thighs he didn't like sitting there in that undignified state in front of his Auntie Daisy. It was she who had made him take his trousers off. He had been all ready for slipping out when her never-resting eyes had spotted the colour of his legs; and anybody could have seen they weren't half as bad as she made out.

'Go on, lad,' Auntie Daisy said. 'Put some elbow-grease into it.'

'I'm gunna be late,' Joby muttered.

'You will be if you don't hurry yourself up. I've never seen such slow motion.'

'Here,' Mona said, coming through into the kitchen, 'I'll get 'em clean.'

She took the scrubbing brush, dipped it in the water and applied Fairy soap. She began to attack Joby's legs until he pulled a face and howled in protest.

'Here, steady on, our Mona. Don't be so rough.'

'I shall have to be rough to get this lot off,' Mona said. 'It's grained in. They look as if you've done a shift down the pit, and you've got tide-marks where your trousers come.'

The brush moved up on to the tender skin of Joby's thighs.

'That's far enough. I'm not having a bath.'

'What's wrong: are you bashful?' She laughed and pretended to tweak at Joby's shirt. 'What you got hiddied under there?'

'Lay off,' Joby said. 'Give over.'

'That'll do, Mona,' Aunt Daisy said primly. 'Are they clean now?'

'They'll do.' Mona passed Joby the towel. 'Here, dry 'em. And do it properly or you'll get chapped. There's a chilly wind today.'

Joby towelled his legs, then jumped down and went into the passage to put his trousers on.

'That's better,' Aunt Daisy observed when she saw him again. 'Your mam 'ud never forgive me if I let you go out looking like summat out o' Foundry Yard.'

Foundry Yard was the town's slum quarter, full of houses with filthy curtainless windows, where slatternly women leant in doorways all day long and hordes of ragamuffin children played in the black dust that was deposited layer after layer, year after year by the foundry over the heavy timber fence. Some of the kids from Foundry Yard came to Joby's old school. One or two were kept clean and tidy by their mothers but most of them turned up in dirty holey jumpers and wore nothing on their feet but battered pumps all the year round. The nit nurse took a particular interest in them and more than one had turned up cropped to the skull after one of her periodic inspections. The houses in Foundry Yard had been condemned for years, but most outsiders were of the opinion that the occupants would turn new council houses into slums in six months. Joby had once made the mistake of swapping some comics with a lad from Foundry Yard. The clout on the ear he got from his mother stopped him from doing it ever again.

'Can I have my Saturday spend?' Joby asked.

Auntie Daisy, in the living-room now and firmly ensconsed in her chair for her after-dinner rest, asked Mona to get her purse from the sideboard drawer.

'How much do you have?' she said, poking with forefinger and thumb among the coins.

'Sixpence. Didn't me mam say?'

'Here y'are, then. Don't spend it all at once.'

Joby took the sixpence. He wasn't saying anything about the shilling his father had given him yesterday. Auntie Daisy was the sort to say he had enough, if she knew about it. With one-and-sixpence all of his own he felt like a millionaire. Why, he could pay into the pictures, buy some sweets and a Dinky car afterwards and still have something left.

He went out and up the road where he found Snap sitting on a wall, waiting for him.

'Where you been?' Snap said. 'I thought you weren't coming.'

'Aw, it was me Auntie Daisy,' Joby said. It was enough, without enlarging. 'Anyway, we're not late.'

'No, but there'll be a big queue.'

'Ne'er mind.'

There was a queue, one of the biggest they had seen for a tuppeny rush, stretching nearly a hundred yards along the pavement from the cinema.

'Think we'll get in?' Snap said.

''Course,' Joby said. 'Have you got enough gelt to go upstairs?'

'Aye, but I shan't be able to get any spice.'

Though it was called the tuppenny rush, it was only the hard seats in the first six rows of stalls that were tuppence on Saturday afternoon. The rest of the seats downstairs were threepence, and in the circle it was fourpence a time. Joby liked going upstairs; it was a bit quieter and even if the kids in front of you bounced about, as they often did when the picture became exciting, you could still see because the seats were steeply raked.

Joby told Snap to keep their places while he went and got some sweets. He queued in the little shop across the street and bought a bar of treacle toffee and twopenn'orth of old-fashioned humbugs – the big buttery kind – and came out as the cinema doors were opened and the line of young people began to move forward.

The cinema was perhaps doing particularly good business this afternoon because they were showing the last episode of their current serial and everybody was eager to know how Flash Gordon would finally deal with that nasty old Ming the Merciless. Perhaps Ming

58

would fall into a bottomless pit of smoke and flames (there were several about) or be struck down by a ray gun. Joby thought it would be a good wheeze to let him get half way across a light-bridge then switch the current off and send him to his death between the high buildings. Or maybe they would put the electrodes to his temples and turn him into a robot as he had done to the good professor early in the serial. Then there were the claymen, slaves of Ming, who materialised out of the walls of the subterranean passages under Ming's palace. Something had to be done to bring them back to normal.

Joby and Snap discussed the possibilities as they moved towards the pay-box, as well as speculating on the feature film – a Buck Jones – and the new serial. For the crafty management, intent upon keeping interest at a peak, were following the last episode of 'Flash Gordon' with the first of 'Jungle Jim'.

Gus Wilson and some of his mates were sitting in the row behind Joby and Snap. There were a couple of girls next to them and Gus kept leaning over and pretending to pass on remarks that Tommy Masterman had made about one of them.

'Ey, he says you've got gorgeous eyes.'

'Gerraway with you,' the lass said.

'He says they're like pools,' Gus said, killing himself: 'football pools.'

'I'm taking no notice,' the lass said.

Tommy was wriggling about with embarrassment.

'Lay off, Gus, will you.'

'Well, you said you liked her, didn't you?'

'I never. When did I say that?'

'Ah, go on, you know you said it.'

'I never did. Me say I liked *her*!'

Joby took another look and saw that the girl was Snotty Marlowe, from Foundry Yard; a thin ugly girl who had a perpetually running nose which she hardly ever bothered to wipe clean.

'Ey, he says will you swap places with me so's he can sit next to you.'

'Tell him to go run up a shutter,' Snotty said.

'He says he'll buy you an ice cream at the interval if you do.'

'She'll have to flippin' well pay for it herself,' Tommy said. 'I've no brass.'

Gus laughed.

'Ey, look who's here. It's Copperknob. You'd better keep that ginger nut down when the picture's on, kid.'

'You can see, can't you?' Snap said.

'If I can't I'll bray your head down into your shoulders,' Gus said; 'like this.'

He clenched his fists, put the left one on top of Snap's head and beat on it with the right.

Snap squirmed out of the way.

'Why can't you leave people alone, Gus Wilson?'

'What d'you mean by that?'

'You're allus making trouble.'

'Oh, am I? Righto, then, I'd better make some for you.'

Joby turned round. He was fed up with Gus spoiling things.

'Look, lay off, Gus, will you?'

'I will if I want to.'

'Well want to, then. We've paid to come in so let us alone.'

'I'm not doing owt to you.'

'You're messing about with Snap.'

'What's that got to do with you?'

'A lot.' ·

'Oh, has it?'

'Aye, it has; so just remember.'

'Why, what will you do?'

'Just carry on and see.'

'Oh,' Gus announced to his friends, 'Joby Weston's a tough guy. I'd better be careful, else he'll bash me up.'

Joby had already turned away. He said nothing to Gus's taunting remark. He wasn't looking for a fight with Gus. He didn't look for fights with anybody but he had had a few in his time. There were occasions when you just had to stick up for yourself.

But Gus didn't press the matter. He had found another amusement. Something whizzed past Joby's ear and a boy several rows away clapped his hand to his neck and looked round. Gus was shooting pellets from a rubber band looped round forefinger and thumb. You made them from cigarette cards, cigarette packets or bus tickets. You could make them from any kind of paper but the heavier it was the better they flew and the more they stung when they hit.

Joby could picture the look of innocence on Gus's face as the victim looked at the back rows, trying to spot the marksman. As soon as he looked round, Gus fired again. He was an expert with a rubber band. The boy reared to his feet, turning and shouting in fury.

61

'Some'dy's shooting pellets back there. Give over, will you!'

The lights faded and the boy sat down again in the darkness. Joby heard a chuckle from the row behind. That Gus! You couldn't have any peace when he was around.

The attendant, a little elderly man, was moving up and down the aisles calling for quiet in a rasping voice. Joby broke the bar of treacle toffee in two and passed half to Snap. They sucked at it as the advertisements for local shops and tradespeople flashed on to the screen. This was a boring part of the show. They saw these same advertisements week after week and nobody would really settle down until the serial began.

The attendant seemed particularly keen this afternoon to get quiet in good time. Unknown to the audience, he had had an interview with the management the day before. There had been some cases of seat-slashing during Saturday matinées and he was directed now to keep order with a firm hand and to eject without argument anyone causing trouble. He was a man who enjoyed his little temporary authority and did not mean to let a crowd of unruly kids deprive him of it and the extra cash it brought in besides his full-time job.

All this was uppermost in his mind when a pellet struck him on the cheek with the force of a hornet's sting. He flashed his torch on the back rows.

'Who's firing pellets?' he demanded. 'Come on, which of you is it?'

There was no reply as the torch beam moved along the rows.

'I can put you all out, y'know,' he said belligerently.

'Ah, go and shove your head up a drainpipe,' a voice bade him from the shadows.

The torch played about and fell on Joby, who at that moment was grinning broadly.

'You there. Was it you?'

Joby blinked in the light of the torch, the grin gone from his face.

'Who, me?'

'Yes, you. Come on out here.'

'I haven't done owt,' Joby said.

'Come on out here or I'll come and pull you out.'

'Oh, cripes,' Joby muttered in disgust.

Gus sniggered as Joby stood up and squeezed out to the aisle.

'I don't know what you're on about,' Joby said. 'I haven't done owt.'

'We'll see about that.' The attendant took Joby by the arm. 'Come on downstairs.'

'But I'm gunna miss the serial,' Joby protested.

'You should ha' thought about that before.'

Joby was marched downstairs into the foyer. The woman in the paybox was cashing up and there were piles of copper and silver set out in rows on the counter.

'Caught one of 'em,' the attendant said in triumph.

'I tell you I haven't done owt,' Joby said yet again.

'Let's see what you've got in your pockets,' the attendant said. 'Come on, turn 'em out.'

Joby did as he was told. It was unfortunate for him that lurking in the lining of one pocket were several

63

pellets left over from last term when the rubber-band craze was at its height. The attendant pounced on them.

'There y'are. What's them if they're not pellets?'

'How can I shoot 'em without a rubber band?' Joby said.

'Ah, you dropped that on the floor inside,' the attendant said.

Joby fumed. He knew he couldn't win. This was grown-ups all over. Find a culprit; it didn't matter if it was the right one or not.

'I've told you it wasn't me,' Joby said. 'I've had them pellets in me pocket for weeks.'

'Are you sure it was him?' the woman in the paybox said, looking doubtfully at Joby.

'Look, I know who it was but it wasn't me,' Joby said, appealing to her.

'Who was it, then?' she asked him.

Joby hesitated. 'I can't split, can I?'

'No, 'cos it was you,' the attendant said.

'Why don't you ask me mate, the lad I was with? He'll tell you it wasn't me.'

'Aw, he'll stick up for you, I reckon. An' anyway, I can't be messing about with you all afternoon, so you can get off home.'

'You mean I can't go back in?'

'No, you can't. And you won't get in next week, neither, if I see you first. Off you go.'

'Give us me money back, then,' Joby said.

'I don't know whether you ought to have it or not, the bother you've caused.'

'You can't refuse him his money, George,' the paybox lady said. She took four pennies off one of the piles and passed them under the glass.

'Here you are. You've made a right mess of it, haven't you?'

Joby sensed she was sorry for him. He said, 'He's got the wrong lad, but it's no use me telling him.'

'Go on, clear off,' the attendant said, 'and don't be so cheeky.'

Joby turned away towards the entrance.

'And don't let me see you here again,' the man called after him.

For a moment Joby was consumed with anger and hatred for the little man.

'I hope you get another pellet in your earhole when you get back inside,' he said.

'Be off with you, you cheeky young devil, before I clatter your face.'

The blind, daft, stupid old keff!

Joby walked sullenly away from the cinema. He smarted at what had happened. He was no angel and he had made his share of mischief; but to carry the can back for something you hadn't done. That hurt.

He didn't know what to do now, either. He couldn't go back to his auntie's before the pictures came out or she would want to know what was wrong; and she was no more likely to believe him than the cinema attendant had. So he had a couple of hours to kill while all his pals were inside watching Flash Gordon. He leant against a wall out of sight of the cinema entrance to think about it. You wouldn't expect Gus to own up to save anybody else. He was probably laughing his hat off thinking about it. Well, he'd saved fourpence and that meant he had one and three left. He could go to the model shop up George Street and buy a Dinky car – or two, if he felt like it. That was some consolation, but not enough to wipe away the sense of injustice and disappointment he felt so strongly. And it wasn't only this week. He was a marked man now. They would probably never let him in again. He was deprived of the pictures on Saturday afternoon unless he caught a bus and went down into Cressley. And that wasn't the same thing. The cinemas in Cressley were too big; he felt lost in them; and he had no mates down there. A fourpenny ticket into the flicks would cost eightpence, counting bus fares, and Snap wouldn't be able to afford that. Nor would he himself in an ordinary week when he had nothing besides his spending money. Yes, it was rotten being an outcast. Especially when you were innocent . . .

He had been standing there several minutes when Mollie Macleod came round the corner. She almost walked straight past him.

'Hello, Joby. What you doing here?'

'Aw, nowt much.'

'I thought you allus went to the pictures Saturday afternoons.'

'I do usually. I didn't feel like it today.'

He didn't know why he was lying because Mollie would probably hear the story from someone else. But he couldn't go into all that now.

'Are you by yourself?'

'Yeh. What are you doing?'

'I'm just off for a bit of a walk.'

'Where to?'

'Just down to the railway. D'you want to come?'

Joby shrugged. 'Might as well'.

He slouched moodily along beside Mollie, his hands shoved deep into his trousers pockets. When they had gone some way he remembered the bag of sweets and took it out and offered it to Mollie.

'Want a spice?'

'Ooh, humbugs! Ta!'

'Take two, if you want,' said Joby, in a fit of generosity.

'I can't eat two at once: they're too big. I'll have another later on.'

Joby popped a humbug into his own mouth and they walked on, cheeks bulging.

Joby had never been alone with Mollie like this before. He knew that if any kids saw them word would get around that he was 'going' with her. But he didn't care. It was better than hanging about on his own. And he found her a more entertaining companion than he would have thought. She talked a lot, but more like a boy than a girl; and she didn't act soft. Now Elsa, he thought, would want protecting; and you would have to behave like a gentleman with her, watching what you said and did. Mollie could stick up for herself and with her you could be natural.

Ah, but if it were Elsa he was walking with now: that would make it all worth while. He felt that he would willingly sacrifice tuppenny rushes for the rest of his life in exchange for a couple of hours of Elsa's willing company. They wouldn't need to talk; they could just walk hand-in-hand through the sunny afternoon. That would be more than enough. Now Mollie, if he offered to take her hand (not that he had any desire to do so), would turn and look at him and laugh out of her mocking eyes and accuse *him* of being soft. And yet she and Elsa belonged to the same mysterious breed.

The mystery of girls was an aspect of Joby's view of life which had developed only recently. Not long ago there had been nothing mysterious about them. They were simply a species of sub-standard boys, who were interested in dolls and sewing and skipping instead of climbing trees and playing football. But they were necessary in the scheme of things because they eventually grew into women and every boy had to have a mother.

The town was soon left behind on this side. They passed an unfinished development of private semi-detached houses where the unmade road petered out into an area littered with piles of new bricks and builders' rubble, and heaps of sand and gravel near a cement-mixer, and crossed a meadow by a path which took them along the rim of the railway cutting. Descending twisting steps into the steep cutting wall, they crossed the railway by a bridge a mile to the west of the one where Joby and Snap had encountered Gus Wilson and his friends.

Mollie seemed to know where she wanted to go and Joby just tagged along. But eventually he said:

'You're not going right down on the riverside, are you?'

'No,' Mollie said, 'not much further. We'll soon be there.'

'Where?' Joby said.

'Where I want to be.'

'I thought you were just going for a walk.'

'I'm looking for something as well.'

'Is it summat you've lost?'

'Well, no. I'm looking for some*body*, really.'

'Who, then?'

'Our kid.'

'Your Agnes?'

'Yeh.'

'What's she doing down here?'

'That's what I want to find out.'

It was all very mysterious, Joby thought. But he had come so far, and he had nothing else to do, so why not go on?

There was a small wood and Mollie took a path which skirted it. Joby followed, hearing in his imagination Gus Wilson's taunting voice:

'He's been in the woods with Mollie Macleod. Ey, what were you doing, then, Joby? Looking for birds' nests?'

There was, apparently, nobody to see them; but Gus sometimes seemed to have spies everywhere. How else could he always know so much?

'Does your Agnes come down here a lot?' he asked.

'Here and other places,' Mollie answered. 'Shurrup now,' she added. 'Don't talk.' She put her finger to her lips. 'Wait here. I'll be back in a tick.'

She went off into the trees and as he looked after her Joby saw that there was a narrow, hardly distinguishable path leading down the slope. She disappeared from sight, reappearing in a few moments to beckon to him furtively. He went towards her and she put her finger to her lips again as he drew near. He jogged along behind her until she suddenly stopped and turned her head to look at him. She pointed down into the trees.

For a few seconds Joby could make nothing out; then all at once he saw them: Agnes Macleod and a chap lying sprawled out in a little hollow. They were kissing. Agnes had her arms clasped tightly round the lad and her frock was pulled up, showing her thighs.

His first instinct was to start up and move away, as though they would feel his eyes on them. But something like fascination held him. He squatted in the bracken and watched the movements of Agnes's bare legs. The boy seemed to be lying between them so that he was held by them as well as Agnes's arms. It occurred to Joby that he couldn't get away if he wanted to, so tightly was Agnes clinging to him.

Mollie touched Joby's arm and he looked round to see her eyes dancing with laughter. She beckoned him away with a jerk of her head and he followed her back along the little path. They went over a stile into a field where she threw herself down among the tall grass by the wall. Joby sat down beside her and began to chew a grass stalk.

'I knew I'd find her,' Mollie said. She seemed very pleased with herself about it.

'Why'd you want to trail all the way down here if you knew where she was?'

'I wanted to make sure.' Mollie turned a look of sly pleasure on Joby. 'Our kid'll have to give me a tanner now so's I won't tell me mam.'

So that was it.

'Suppose she gives you a clout instead, for spying on her?'

'She daren't do that. She knows I'll tell me mam an' then she'll get a leatherin'. She's been told to leave the lads alone, but she can't keep away from 'em.'

'Have you had any money out of her before?'

'Many a time. 'Fact, I'm thinking of putting the price up to a bob. She'll have more money when she starts working.' She looked sidelong at Joby. 'Could you see what they were doing?'

Joby shrugged. He felt a mixture of fascination and revulsion as an image of Agnes and the boy sprang into his mind.

'Kissing one another.'

'Is that all?' Mollie said.

'I dunno.' Joby plucked at the grass, feeling his face reddening.

'I'll bet you don't know the difference between men and women,' Mollie said.

''Course I do,' Joby said, mustering all the scorn he could.

'Well, what is it, then?'

'Well . . . well, women have longer hair than men.'

Mollie exploded with laughter and put her hands over her eyes. 'Longer hair!' She thought that was very funny. She uncovered her face. 'Is that all, then?'

'No, there's other things.'

'What other things?'

'I don't know the words,' Joby muttered. He did know a few dirty ones but he wasn't going to say them to Mollie.

Mollie was looking at him in a queer way.

71

'If I show you will you show me?'

'What for?'

'You'd like to know, wouldn't you?'

He shrugged. 'Mebbe.' He wished she wouldn't look at him. He couldn't look at her. His cheeks were burning like fire.

'You're blushing,' Mollie said.

'Well, what if I am?'

'You're scared, that's why.'

'I'm not scared,' Joby said. 'I got thrown out of the pictures this afternoon.'

'What for?'

'Shooting pellets at the attendant.'

Mollie didn't appear to be impressed.

'I'll go first if you'll go second.'

'What if somebody comes?'

'Nobody can see us here. Come on, then; will you promise?'

'I'm thinking about it,' Joby said.

5

Joby was alone when he came back up into town later that afternoon. He didn't want to be seen with Mollie and he had run on ahead of her. The pictures were just coming out, a flood of kids pouring out of the building into the narrow street. Some of the young ones were reluctant to make the transition back to reality. They galloped off on imaginary horses with great slapping of their own backsides and pointing two fingers of one hand to shoot one another down. Joby caught sight of Snap's ginger hair at the same time as Snap saw him.

'Where you been, Joby?'

'Oh, just walking round. Was it a good show?'

'Yeh, right good. Hard lines you getting chucked out like that.'

'I told him it wasn't me but he wouldn't believe me. Daft old devil. Did Gus make any more trouble after?'

Snap shook his head. 'Naw.'

'No,' Joby said, 'he's too crafty to give the game away like that.'

'He was on to me a bit,' Snap said. 'Flicking me ear, an' all that.'

'Aye, he would.'

Somebody bumped against Joby and sent him reeling forward into Snap, who prevented him from falling down.

'Here, watch where you're going, can't you?'

'Oh, sorry, Joby,' Gus Wilson said.

Joby righted himself and turned to see the false innocence on Gus's face.

'What d'you mean "sorry"? You did that on purpose.'

'I never did.'

'No, and I don't suppose you let me take the blame and get chucked out of the pictures, either?'

'It's not my fault if you get chucked out.'

'It is when it should ha' been you.'

'Why me, then?'

'Because you shot the pellet and gave him the cheek. It was you he was after, but he picked me instead.'

'Hard lines, then,' Gus said.

'Yeh, hard lines. You won't find that big shot Gus Wilson owning up to what he's done. He'd rather let some'dy else take the blame.'

The tension was rising. Joby could feel it in the quickening of his pulse. He saw sidelong glances thrown at Gus to see how he would react. Gus had a reputation to keep up. Another few words and he would be forced to do something or appear to back down. He was, then, picking a fight with Gus; a fight he thought he couldn't win. But he didn't care now. He had had enough of dancing to Gus's tune. He was mad.

Snap plucked at his sleeve. 'Come on, Joby; let's go.'

Joby answered him over his shoulder. 'You buzz off, if you want to. I'm talking to Big Shot Wilson.'

74

'You wanna be careful who you're calling,' Gus said.

'Why?' Joby said.

'Else you might get bashed.'

'Fetch your army an' start bashing.'

'I don't need any army to bash you, Weston.'

Gus pushed him on the shoulder. It was the spark needed to explode Joby's smouldering temper. He swung with his right fist and caught Gus on the cheek then danced back with his head down, fists at the ready. A circle of lads had formed round them at the first sign of trouble and he felt somebody's toe under his heel and interfering hands trying to push him back into the middle of the ring. He drove backwards with his elbow.

'Give us some room, can't you?'

Space was what he needed. It was his only hope. He was lighter than Gus and quicker on his feet. But if once Gus grappled with him and got him down weight would finish him.

Gus's reaction was quick and his first blow more accurate than Joby's. Tears sprang to Joby's eyes as his nose seemed to swell to enormous proportions. Forgetting his own tactics, he flew at Gus with a hail of blows, their very fury driving Gus back some way. He covered his face, taking Joby's onslaught on his forearms. Joby swung under Gus's guard, aiming between his ribs with the idea of winding him, and as his own guard fell a clout from Gus took him on the ear and sent him reeling. He felt a couple of boys slip out from behind him and then his back was against the wall.

Gus rushed him in the same moment the old attendant reached them and pushed through the circle to grasp them by their jackets and hold them apart.

'That's enough o' that! Stop it off now!' He looked at Joby. 'You causin' trouble again, eh? I thought I told you to clear off home long since?'

'You don't own the street, do you?' Joby said.

'I'll tell you what, though,' the attendant said, 'I own a good clout on the earhole 'at I'll give you in a minute.'

He pushed them both away from him.

'Now get off home, the lot of you.'

Joby found himself walking away at Gus's side.

'And don't forget what I told you,' the attendant shouted after him. 'You've no need to come back next week 'cos you won't get in.'

Joby swung round and put his hand to the side of his mouth. 'Go an' boil your fat head, you silly old bugger!'

Turning back he cannoned into a well dressed middle-aged woman who stood and looked after him with a shocked face as he and Gus emerged into the High Street where they paused on the edge of the pavement. They couldn't fight here. Not that Joby wanted to carry on, anyway. He had relieved his feelings and shown he wasn't scared of standing up to Gus. It was enough.

'Your mate seems to have cleared off,' Tommy Masterman said.

'He won't be far away,' Joby said.

'I wouldn't call *him* a mate. He clears off as soon as there's any trouble.'

'Well he doesn't go round making it for other

people,' Joby said; 'and that's summat. Anyway, nobody's asking what you think.'

Tommy gave an elaborate shrug. 'Okay; if you wanna be like that.'

'Yeh, I do,' Joby said. He turned away from them and walked off into the shopping crowds.

It was tea-time and he would be expected at his Auntie Daisy's. But he didn't want to go there. After all the complications and misunderstandings of the afternoon he wanted the warmth of home. He wanted to have a tea made by his mother and eat it in her company. He was missing her now, more acutely than at any time earlier in the week, and he wished he was allowed to go and see her.

He went home anyway and found his father about to have his own tea. He had laid the table with the bare necessities: a plate and a fork and his mug, the sugar-bowl and some butter still in its wrapping, and a partly used loaf and the breadknife. The tablecloth had stains on it and looked as if it had been in use all week. While the kettle came to the boil on the gas-ring Weston was opening a tin of salmon. He was in his shirtsleeves and a pullover and flannel trousers. He glanced over his shoulder as Joby went in.

'Hello, Joby. How you doing?'

'Oh, not bad.'

Joby leaned against a chair and watched his father wrestle with the tin. The opener he was using was a gadget that had never been much good and Weston had threatened many a time to chuck it out and get a simple old-fashioned one.

'Is your stomach better?' Joby asked.

'What? Oh, aye. Yes, it's all right now.'

'Have you been to see me mam?'

'Aye, yes. She's sitting up and taking notice a bit now. She said to tell you to be a good lad and she won't be long as she's home.'

'I wish I could go and see her.'

'Aye, but it's against the rules, lad.'

Weston got the tin open and pushed the contents out on to a plate with a knife. Then he poured boiling water into the teapot.

'Have you had your tea, then?'

'No.'

'Your Auntie Daisy'll have it ready for you, won't she?'

'I expect so.'

'You won't want to keep her waiting, y'know.'

'Can't I stop an' have me tea with you?'

His father looked at him directly for the first time since he had come in.

'What about your auntie?'

'She won't have cooked anything to spoil.'

'No, I suppose not. Still, you don't want to put her about, y'know. It's very kind of her to have you while your mam's away. We don't want to offend her.'

'I'd rather stop here for me tea,' Joby said.

His father hesitated.

'Oh, well, I reckon it'll be all right for once. D'you fancy some salmon? There's enough here for two and it'll help finish the tin afore it goes off . . . Get yourself some tackle out, then. It's ready otherwise.'

There was a small diversion before they could start,

for Weston had forgotten to put tea into the pot, which meant boiling some more water. He got up, muttering about absent-mindedness, and cut some bread while they waited. Then they sat down on opposite sides of the table and began to eat in a long silence that was eventually broken by Joby saying:

'I got thrown out of the pictures this aft., Dad.'

'Oh aye?'

Joby wondered if his father could have heard what he'd said.

'It wasn't my fault, though. I wasn't doing owt. It was Gus Wilson, y'see. He was firing pellets with a rubber band and the attendant thought it was me and made me go out. He wouldn't take any notice of what I said.'

'You'll have to behave yourself, y'know,' Weston said, 'else they'll be stopping you going.'

'They've told me I can't go any more now. And it wasn't me at all. It was Gus Wilson.'

'Gus?'

'His real name's John, only everybody calls him Gus. I don't know why.'

'I think I know his father. He comes down to t'club.'

Joby's father reached for the plate of salmon. He was about to push what was left on to his own plate when he stopped.

'D'you fancy a bit more?'

'No. I've had enough.'

Weston emptied the plate.

'Very tasty now and again, a bit o' salmon. Been a pity to open that big tin just for me, though.'

Joby watched his father eating. He was puzzled. He

79

had expected him to be angry about the pictures episode until it was made clear that he, Joby, was innocent. But now his dad seemed to think he'd caused the trouble anyway, yet he didn't apparently mind.

'Are you worried about summat, Dad?' he asked, and Weston glanced at him.

'Well, I have summat on me mind a bit.'

A spasm of fear stabbed Joby's heart. The world which had swallowed his mother was unknown and terrifying, full of dark secrets. He distrusted it just as he distrusted the evasions of grown-ups when they mentioned it. Suppose he were to be told one day that his mother was never coming back? Oh, it was fantastic, but it *could* happen. Look at Mary Brotherton. Her mother had gone into hospital and Mary had never seen her again. That was only last year and now Mary lived with an auntie all the time and her younger sister and baby brother lived somewhere else.

He swallowed hard and forced the question.

'Is it about me mam?'

'No . . . no, she's all right. No, it's about a little job at work, that's all.'

Joby didn't know whether to believe him or not. He hadn't really heard anything Joby had said since coming in.

They sat in silence for some time, Weston smoking and looking into the low fire which burned in the open grate.

'Is there a cricket match down in the field tonight?' Joby asked presently.

'Happen so. Why?'

'I thought you might be going to watch it.'

'I can't tonight,' Weston said. 'I've to go and pay me sick-club dues.'

Joby relapsed into silence. The late afternoon sun poured into the room through the smaller window and he looked out at the blue sky over the roof-tops of the houses opposite.

'Don't you think it's time you were letting your Auntie Daisy know where you've got to?'

'Yeh, I suppose so.'

'Aye,' Weston said absently, 'I should get off an' tell her where you've been.'

Joby got up and wandered to the door.

'Dad.'

'Eh?'

'About the pictures. I was wondering. If you went to see the attendant and told him it wasn't me what caused the trouble they'd happen let me in next week.'

'Oh, I shouldn't worry about that,' Weston said. 'It'll all come out in the wash . . . Off you go to your Auntie Daisy's. She'll be wondering.'

'I'll be seeing you, then.'

'Aye, so long, Joby. Be a good lad and do as your auntie tells you.'

What did he want? Joby asked himself as he walked away from the house. What was it he was looking for? Did he really believe his mother was in danger, that she wasn't coming back to make life as before? He didn't know what he did believe. Somehow the events of the afternoon had contracted themselves into a sharp point of loneliness and uncertainty which ripped a small tear in the protective fabric of his world. So that now he looked through the tear at his world and

81

though it seemed in almost every way the same it was in fact different. The streets, the houses, the shops of the town where he had been born and lived all his life, that he knew better than any streets or houses or shops anywhere – they were all the same as before, yet different because he was looking at them through the tear. He wanted, he *needed* now, a grown-up whom he could trust and who would, if only for a few minutes, talk to him directly, really talk to him, person to person, without evasions or mention of rules or fobbing him off because he wouldn't understand. He *could* understand if only he had the chance. But it seemed there was only one person who would even make the attempt to talk to him like that, and she wasn't here and he couldn't get to her.

The High Street was quieter now; people had finished their week-end shopping and the stores were closing. He wondered if there was still time for him to buy the Dinky cars he wanted from the model shop. He fingered the money in his pocket as a double-deck bus whooshed by close to the pavement. He felt the draught of its passing round his legs and looked after it as it stopped a little farther up the road. It was going to Cressley . . .

As he thought this the idea of the money and the bus clicked together in Joby's mind and started him running up the pavement to leap on to the platform as the bus began to move. The back of the driver's head seemed familiar. Joby gave him only a quick glance before running up the steps to the upper deck. If it was Uncle Ted he might have seen him on the pavement as the bus passed; but he wouldn't know he had got on.

Ten minutes later he was dropping off the bus in the middle of Cressley. He was on the edge of the market and he strolled through the lanes of empty stalls where dirty sheets of newspaper and orange-wrappings littered the cobbles – all the debris of the day's trading. A few stall-holders hung on there, selling the last of their perishable goods to women who knew the dodge of shopping late and filled bags with fruit and vegetables at a fraction of their midday prices.

The market was a forlorn place at this time of day and Joby didn't linger. On the other side he found himself on the road that led past the infirmary and he walked along it with no idea in his mind beyond the knowledge that each step took him a little nearer his mother. There were two notices on the gate pillars: one which told you this was the infirmary and the other giving a speed limit for motor vehicles of 10 m.p.h. Beyond the trees of the drive the great walls of the hospital reared up, pierced by hundreds of windows. There were balconies too and long glass corridors joining the separate buildings. This, it struck Joby, was a place that could never stop working; a great repair shop for human beings. Sometimes people went in and were mended as good as new. Sometimes they were never properly well again. Sometimes they went in and didn't come out, because people were not like motor cars and nobody knew everything about them.

An ambulance turned the corner and came down the drive. Joby stood aside and watched it pass by and move away down the hill towards the centre of town. A moment later he was walking up the way the ambulance had come, towards the main entrance of the hospital.

It was ridiculously easy to get inside the hospital, because there was no one about to stop him. There must be people – the buildings were surely full of them – but he could see nobody. And nobody apparently noticed him as he crossed the courtyard and went up the steps to the doors. He looked in through the glass of the doors for a time before pushing them open and stepping inside. The hall was a vast place with a tiled floor and long leather-covered benches. Two nurses passed through on the far side and their soft, re-strained laughter echoed up in the high vaulted ceiling. Joby stood back behind a pillar, though why he was hiding from them or what he hoped to achieve here he didn't know.

When the nurses had gone he waited a minute then ventured a few steps into the open hall. There were a lot of doors about and corridors leading away into the heart of the building. On one wall, between two high narrow windows, hung an oil painting of a man with glasses and a big moustache. He wore a mayor's gold chain over the shoulders of his dark high-fronted suit. There were also some polished brass plates with letter-ing on them that Joby couldn't read because they were fixed too high on the walls.

He was moving towards one of the plaques to see what was written on it and was caught so, isolated in the middle of the great hall, when a swing door with a round window was pushed back and a stout grey-haired woman in a pink-and-white nursing uniform walked briskly through. He thought at first she hadn't seen him; then she changed course and came towards him, her voice echoing like those of the other nurses as she started to speak to him from twenty feet away.

'Now, young man, what do you want?'

Her eyes glinted behind her rimless glasses; with humour or irritation, Joby couldn't tell. He stammered as he began speaking and his heart was knocking uncomfortably.

'I was looking for me mother.'

'Are you with her?'

'No, I'm on me own.'

Her glance flicked over him, taking all in.

'Have you been sent here for treatment? Is there something wrong with you?'

Joby shook his head. 'No, I'm just looking for me mam.'

'Is your mother a patient here?'

'Yes, she's inside.'

'Ah, I see. Well, I'm afraid you can't see her. Visiting hours are over, and little boys aren't allowed in anyway. What's her name?'

'Mrs Weston . . . I wanted to find out how she was going on, so I came up.'

'Hasn't anybody visited her?'

'Me dad comes,' Joby said. 'He came today.'

'Well, hasn't he told you how she is?'

'He says she's all right; but I wanted to find out for myself.'

The nurse looked at him for a long moment until Joby felt himself blushing under her gaze and his heart beat faster still. She was going to tell him to go: he'd no business here, meddling into grown-up affairs. Instead she said:

'You wait here. Don't go wandering off.'

She walked away across the hall, round a corner, and out of sight. Joby waited, wondering where she had gone and what she was going to do. A stretcher came by, rolling noiselessly on rubber wheels, pushed by a man in a white tunic. There was someone on the stretcher, lying very still with blankets drawn right up to the chin. His mother must have looked like that after her operation; a white unconscious face protruding from taut blankets. His mother helpless in the hands of people whose job it was to look after her, though they didn't really care. How could they? They didn't know her. What was his mother to them except one of hundreds of patients?

He had no means of knowing how long he stood in the huge empty hall; but as he waited through the dragging minutes for the nurse to return the strangeness and impersonality of the hospital seemed a tangible weight that bore down oppressively upon him. He felt very far from home, not only in terms of exaggerated distance but in his knowledge that for the first time in his life he could not think of home as a secure embracing whole. It was incomplete. The heart had been taken out of it. It was a spick and span house in which a solitary pre-occupied man laid a table with the bare necessities for a lonely meal.

The vision frightened Joby. He wanted to run from it and from all the other images of the day that flashed through his mind: Agnes Macleod lying with the boy in the wood; the mocking, laughing face of her sister

Mollie as she crouched in the tall grass; the fight with Gus, and the shame of being sent out of the cinema. He wanted to run from it all into the warm secure heart of life. His heart fluttered. He felt the trembling of his limbs and became aware that his entire body was quivering and painfully tensed, drawn out quivering and taut as though poised on the edge of flight.

So that when the hand fell on his shoulder from behind he almost screamed in terror. The man's uniform, seen in one flashing glimpse, was instantly translated into the symbol of unrelenting authority. He twisted free, lashing out with one arm, and ran for the entrance. He heard the man call out before the heavy door closed behind him but he ran on, hurtling headlong across the yard and down the drive. Only when he was clear of the hospital grounds did he stop and lean against a wall, holding his arms tightly folded across his chest as though to press out the pain from his lungs.

It was a few moments later that he began to cry. He was alone in the road but he was beyond caring who saw him weep and past the shame of weeping at all. For a while it was as though his mother were actually dead. He was drunk with grief. He staggered under it, unable to walk more than half a dozen steps at a time. In this way, taking a few paces, then stopping to hide his face in his arms against the wall, he went down the deserted road and into the town.

His Aunt Daisy was livid with rage. She banged about in her anger, making him supper she said he didn't deserve while he sat up to the table, mute and white-faced, the words of explanation locking deeper and deeper in him the more she stormed on. She'd been worried sick, she said, having the responsibility of him and not knowing where he was. Mona had been out all round the town looking for him and they had been on the point of going to the police. Mona was on her way out to look for his father again when she met him coming along the street 'as though he had all the time in the world.' He had hung about at the end of the road for half an hour after walking home from Cressley across the fields, not wanting to go back to his auntie's, his reluctance only partly composed of the fear of the row he would get into for being late.

'And I hear you got sent out of the pictures this afternoon,' Aunt Daisy said.

Joby didn't trouble himself with how she had got to know. Grown-ups had spies everywhere.

'It wasn't my fault,' he said.

'No, and I reckon stopping out till this hour wasn't your fault either?'

Joby sank into silence again, looking at the two slices of bread and dripping on the plate in front of him. He took a bite from one of them. It tasted dry and unpalatable. He chewed, feeling that he would never be able to swallow it.

'I allus thought you were a well-behaved lad 'at did as he was told,' Aunt Daisy was saying. 'But I'm beginning to revise me ideas a bit. We'll see what your dad has to say about it. If you're going to carry on like this you'll be better off at home with him . . . Get your supper eaten. It's time you were in bed.'

Joby pushed the plate away. 'I don't want it.'

88

'After you've sat there and watched me get it ready!'

Joby put his head down in his hands. He wouldn't cry, he wouldn't.

'Aw, leave him alone a bit, Mam,' Mona said. 'Can't you see he's all upset?'

'An' I'm not, I suppose?' Aunt Daisy said. 'Sitting here hour after hour wondering where he can be, if he's had an accident or summat.'

'Are you upset about summat, Joby?' Mona asked, putting her hand on his shoulder. 'You haven't got into trouble or owt, have you?'

'No.' Joby turned his face away. He wasn't going to bare himself now in front of Aunt Daisy, who had put him in the wrong from the beginning. Grown-ups – he hated them all. All except one; and he wouldn't talk about her to anybody.

6

Aunt Daisy made Joby go to chapel twice with her the next day, Sunday. Aunt Daisy's chapel was rather extreme and had a mission-hall atmosphere. Its congregation were mostly 'converted' people who, further than merely worshipping regularly, had at some service – probably during a special week-end evangelical rally – stood up in front of everybody and gone forward to kneel before the pulpit and pledge themselves to the Lord. Some of them were very vocal in their appreciation of the sermons and particularly stirring passages would move them to cries of 'Hallelujah!' and 'Praise the Lord!' They were people who, according to Aunt Daisy, had turned their backs on the shams and pretences and lip service of church worship and 'taken Christ into their daily lives.' Joby sometimes wondered if this had the effect on most people that it seemed to have on Aunt Daisy, which was not uplifting and joyful so much as provident of a state of personal salvation from which the omissions and shortcomings of others could be seen the more clearly and commented upon with sour intolerance.

The preacher in the morning was a Mr Featherstonhaugh, whom Aunt Daisy spoke highly of. He was a small man and not much of him was visible above the pulpit except a round shiny bald head and a bulbous open-pored nose from which sprouted a forest of curly grey hairs. What he lacked in physical stature he made up for in the force of his delivery and his conviction in what he had to say. Mr Featherstonhaugh's sermon was topical. He did not believe that war was either necessary or inevitable. He did not believe there would be a war though there were people here in our own country who by rashness of speech and action were doing their best to bring one about. He took as his text St Matthew, Chapter 5, verses 8 and 9: *Blessed are the pure in heart: for they shall see God. Blessed are the peacemakers: for they shall be called the children of God.* He spoke, as Aunt Daisy pointed out, without a scrap of paper in front of him except the Bible (it was to her a sign of ability in a preacher) and went on for an hour while Joby fidgeted on the hard shiny seat between the absorbed gaze of Aunt Daisy on one side and the dull, vacuous stare of Mona on the other with nothing to look at but his hands, his pink scrubbed knees, the dust motes dancing in the beams of sunlight and the shining pate of Mr Feathertsonhaugh bobbing on the rim of the pulpit while his occasional points of forceful rhetoric brought forth the responses of the less inhibited faithful: *Hallelujah! . . . Praise the Lord!*

There was an unfortunate interruption when an old lady, apparently subject to fainting fits, passed out at the back of the hall and had to be carried out into the fresh air with a great deal of banging and thumping and shuffling of feet while the rest of the congregation pretended not to notice. But Mr Featherstonhaugh took it in his stride and with a brief passing word about 'our unfortunate sister' plunged back into the theme of his sermon. Too far back for Joby's liking, for he spent fifteen minutes recapping points made before the interruption, evidently to ensure no loss of continuity or flow in the journey to his peroration.

It was all very successful and there was no doubt it would in other surroundings have merited a prolonged round of applause. As it was, the fortunate few – Aunt Daisy among them – who knew Mr Featherstonhaugh personally hung back after the meeting to congratulate him. Mr Featherstonhaugh shook hands with Aunt Daisy and said how nice it was to see her again. He smiled vaguely at Mona and put his hand on Joby's head and enquired if he was a member of the League of Junior Evangelists. When Joby said no Mr Featherstonhaugh produced a collection of printed leaflets from his attaché case which he said would tell Joby all about it. On looking at them later Joby found they were mostly a long series of questions the answering of which involved the reading of the New Testament. If you sent in the answers to the League's headquarters in London you received in return a small de-luxe edition of the New Testament with coloured illustrations and a sticker which certified that you were a member and dedicated to furthering the aims of the League and abiding by its precepts. Joby, who liked both reading and being a member of organisations and societies (he had started several secret societies himself), thought it looked fun and wished he could have usefully occupied his time doing the questions during Mr Featherston-haugh's sermon.

Joby's father came to Aunt Daisy's at dinnertime and joined them in the boiled potatoes, cauliflower and cold cuts from Saturday's joint which was all Aunt Daisy's Sunday-morning chapel-going allowed her to get ready. There were only the four of them to sit down. Uncle Ted was doing a Sunday shift, which was against Aunt Daisy's principles but unavoidable in his job. Joby hoped that Aunt Daisy might have let off enough steam last night to think it unnecessary to mention his escapade to his father. But he had reckoned without her sense of duty and her liking for people to know the circumstances in which she did them a good turn. She told Weston what had happened as she served the dinner.

'Well he come and asked me if he could have his tea with me, Daisy; and I sent him off up here straight after to tell you where he'd been.'

'It took him a long time to get here,' Aunt Daisy said, 'It was nearly ten o'clock by the time he walked in.'

'And where the hummer had you been till that time, then?' Weston demanded, with more of irritation in his voice than anger.

'Oh, just hanging about,' Joby muttered.

'Didn't I tell you to come straight up here and tell your Auntie Daisy where you'd been?'

'Yes.'

'And why didn't you, then?'

'I forgot.'

Aunt Daisy snorted and Weston waved his knife at Joby. 'You'd better behave yourself in future. I've a good mind to give you a hiding. Upsetting your Auntie

Daisy like that when she's doing all she can to help us. It's bad enough your mam being away without you causing trouble at home. Y'hear what I'm saying?'

Joby said yes.

'Aye, well just think on. 'Else you'll be feeling the flat of my hand.'

'I think he's worried about his mam,' Mona said. 'Aren't you, Joby?'

'What's he want to be worried about her for?' Weston said. 'I've told him she's going on all right. More likely she'll be worried about him when she gets to know what he's been up to.'

'You won't tell her, will you, Dad?' Joby said.

'What have I to tell her if she asks me if you've been a good lad?'

'I don't want her to get upset.'

'Why didn't you think of that before, eh?'

There was a falseness in this adult logic that Joby couldn't quite isolate. But it seemed most people were possessed of a sense of duty whose exercise made things unpleasant for somebody else.

'Are you going to see her this afternoon?'

'I am. And your Auntie Daisy's going with me.'

Joby thought for a moment.

'If I write her a letter will you give it to her for me?'

'All right,' Weston conceded.

'Then she might write me one back.'

'Aye, happen so.'

'We'd better get a move on if we're going up there,' Aunt Daisy said. 'We don't want to be late.'

'I'll see to the washing-up,' Mona said. 'You needn't bother about that.'

94

'You wash and I'll dry,' Joby's father said. 'Then we'll be done twice as sharp. Anyway, there's no need to rush. There's a bus at two that'll get us there in ample time.'

'Oh, well,' Aunt Daisy said, 'in that case I'll have a lie-down for ten minutes. I do like a lie-down on a Sunday afternoon.'

As soon as the meal was over Aunt Daisy retired upstairs for her nap and Joby's father followed Mona into the kitchen to wash up. Joby sat at the table with a sheet of writing-paper and chewed the end of his pencil as he thought out the letter to his mother. When he had finished he slipped the letter into the envelope Mona had given him and went to hand it to his father so that he wouldn't forget it. He stopped in the passage at the foot of the stairs to stick down the flap of the envelope and rest it against the wall while he wrote 'Mam' on the outside. He could hear his father and Mona talking in the kitchen and there was a sudden little cry and a giggle from Mona, as though she were being tickled.

'Look, behave yourself; you'll get us both into bother.'

Joby had never heard Mona speak like that to his father. He didn't think they knew he was so near. The scullery door was slightly ajar and he stepped across the thick listing rug at the bottom of the stairs and looked through the crack as Mona said, 'Look, me mam'll be down in a minute, and there's Joby only next door.'

'We're all right for a minute,' Weston said. 'What you scared of?'

95

Joby was looking at Uncle Ted's big shaving-mirror hanging on the scullery wall and the reflection in it of his father and Mona standing with their faces together. His father kissed Mona on the mouth before she pushed him away with 'Give it up, now; don't be so daft.'

Joby went quietly back into the living-room. He had just sat down and picked up his comic when Mona came through.

'Oh, have you finished your letter, then? That didn't take long.'

'It's only a short one,' Joby said.

'I hope there's no spelling mistakes in it.'

'I'm a good speller,' Joby said. 'I'm always top of the class in spelling.'

'I never could spell,' Mona admitted. 'and I hate writing letters. You can never say things properly in a letter.'

'Where's me dad?' Joby asked.

'He's just having a wash under the tap. What are we going to do this afternoon? If we went down on the bus with me mam and your dad we could go and have a walk round the park while they were in hospital.'

'I thought me Auntie Daisy said I'd got to go to Sunday School?'

'Oh, yeh; I'd forgotten about that. Well, you'd better go, hadn't you? You won't get a prize if you keep missing.'

'I don't want to go, though,' Joby said.

Weston came through, rubbing towel fluff off his chin with the back of his hand.

'Don't want to what? It's about time you did as you

96

were told, never mind saying what you want and don't want. Have you got that letter done?'

Joby handed it to him.

'You won't forget to give it to her, will you? And ask her to write me one back?'

'I don't know as she'll have time to be writing letters with visitors there,' Weston said. 'Happen she'll write one when we've gone and send it on next time.'

'Ask her if she knows when she's coming home.'

'I'll see if she's got to know owt about it.'

Joby left the house as his Aunt Daisy's heavy, deliberate tread was heard on the stairs and walked towards the town. The Sunday School he went to was not at Aunt Daisy's chapel but their own; or what his mother called their own though she didn't go very often now and his father had never gone much at all. On the way he met Gus Wilson and Tommy Masterman. They were sitting on a wall taking swigs alternately from a pint bottle of lemonade. Neither Gus nor Tommy went to Sunday School and Joby envied them for their freedom of the gloriously bright afternoon. He couldn't avoid passing them and he wondered if they had known he would be coming this way and were waiting to make him finish yesterday's fight. But their greetings seemed friendly enough.

'Hi, Joby. Where you going?'

'Sunday School.'

'What for?'

''Cos I have to.'

'Have you seen that mate of yours, Snap?'

Joby wasn't so sure Snap was a mate of his now, after

97

the way he had run off at the first sign of trouble yesterday afternoon.

'I saw him yesterday afternoon. Why?'

'Have you heard about his uncle?'

'No. What about him?'

'He's hung hisself.'

This was surely one of Gus's funny jokes.

'You're kidding,' he said; but as he looked from Gus to Tommy he had a feeling they weren't for once.

Gus shook his head. 'Cross me heart. He hung hisself last night in the lav. with his braces.'

'Well . . . what did he want to do that for?'

'How do I know? Mebbe he left a note and they'll find out from that.'

Joby didn't go to Snap's house much and he had seen Snap's uncle only a few times. He knew him as a thin dark man, going prematurely bald, who never had much to say except when he was arguing with Snap's father or, apparently, telling Snap stories about the Spanish war. Though you never knew how much of that Snap had been told and how much had grown out of his imagination.

'They say it was Snap 'at found him,' Gus said. 'He went out for a pee and when he opened the lav. door there he was, hanging up by his braces.' He held out the lemonade bottle to Joby. 'Wanna swig?'

Joby shook his head.

'Is'll have to go. Me dad and me Auntie Daisy 'ull be coming on here in a minute and I'm supposed to be at Sunday School.'

Gus handed the bottle to Tommy and jumped off the wall.

'We'll walk on with you.'

They went a little way, walking three abreast where the pavement was wide enough, and Tommy hopping in and out of the gutter where it wasn't.

Fancy, though, Snap's uncle killing himself . . . Why should he want to do that? Why should anybody want to do it? And Snap finding him. That would be horrible . . .

'I wouldn't hang meself if I wanted to do meself in,' Gus said. 'Not with me braces, anyway. When they hang a murderer they have a big knot in the rope and that breaks his neck as soon as he drops through the trap. You can't do that with braces; you just throttle yourself, ever so slow.'

'I'd chuck meself under a train,' Tommy said.

'An' be chopped into little bits?'

'Well, it's quick, anyway.'

'Shooting yerself's best,' Gus said. He pointed two fingers at the side of his head. 'Just pull the trigger and it's all over. Bang!'

'What if you can't get a gun, though?'

'Well, I'd jump off a high building.'

'What about drowning?'

'Naw, you might change your mind and try to swim out. Which way would you do it, Joby?'

'I don't know.'

'What about taking a lot of aspirins afore you go to bed?' Tommy said. 'Then you'd just die in your sleep.'

'Time to change your mind again.'

'Well, then there's gassing yourself.'

'Yeh, that's not bad. I hate the stink of gas, though.'

'And cutting your throat from ear to ear.'

'Mebbe you wouldn't have the guts to hurt yourself like that.'

'You need guts to commit suicide at all.'

'Naw,' Gus said, 'it's the coward's way out.'

'I don't think Snap's uncle was a coward,' Joby said.

'Why'd he kill hisself, then?'

'Well, he went to fight in Spain. didn't he, and he'd no need to do that?'

'Mebbe he didn't know how rough it was gunna be.'

'Well, nobody knows why he killed himself, do they?'

'Not unless he wrote a letter. Lots o' people write letters when they do theirselves in.'

'Not everybody.'

'No, but most of 'em.'

They had reached the High Street. The Wesleyan Chapel with its huge porticoed front stood two hundred yards up the road. Sunday School was held in a separate building, behind the chapel, that was also let out for wedding receptions, concerts and amateur dramatics. Joby saw one of his teachers, Miss Jessop, walking very straight, in a grey costume and a hat with artificial flowers on it, pass along the opposite pavement. Miss Jessop was very fond of her hats and she had a lot. They were usually striking and often frivolous and Joby could never reconcile this taste with Miss Jessop's severe manner and her lack of a sense of humour.

'Is'll have to be going,' Joby said, 'else I'll be late.'

'Why don't you come with us instead?' Gus said.

'Where to?'

'Down the park in Cressley. There'll be a band

100

playing this aft. Nobody'll know if you don't go, will they?'

No, there was really no one to question his absence.

'Is'll have to make sure I'm back in good time, if I do.'

'We shan't be late. Come on. Why don't you?' Gus glanced round. 'Look, there's a bus coming now. Let's catch it.'

He and Tommy darted away to the bus stop and after a second's hesitation Joby followed them. They reached the bus as it came to a halt and on a sudden thought Joby threw a glance at the cab. But he was lucky again: it wasn't Uncle Ted. He would have to be careful coming back, he thought, and also watch out for his dad and Auntie Daisy down in Cressley. Otherwise no one would know he had stayed away from Sunday School. It was too much anyway for him to go there in the afternoon and to morning and evening services as well. His mother wouldn't have made him do it. Only his Aunt Daisy would expect all that.

They sat upstairs, at the back, and passed the lemonade bottle round. This time Joby didn't refuse a drink. The lemonade was tepid now and most of its fizz had gone. Still, it wet your throat. Gus and Tommy produced a quarter-pound block of chocolate each and offered Joby some. When he said they seemed to have plenty of money to throw about they grinned and Gus said he'd won the football pools.

The bus moved down the valley into Cressley. The sun through its windows was hot on Joby's face and he began to sweat a little. He thought it was very pleasant being accepted by Gus and Tommy in this way and wondered what he'd done to deserve it. Perhaps he had increased Gus's respect by sticking up to him and Gus wanted anybody like that on his side. Anyway, it was all right. Presently he thought about Snap and his uncle again. Well, Snap would really have something to talk about now. If he felt like it.

* * *

He made sure he wasn't late for tea; even so, Aunt Daisy was short with him.

'Where've you been till this time?'

He thought for a moment he'd been found out and wondered if he was blushing and giving himself away.

'I went for a walk after Sunday School.'

'Well, get your tea, then we can wash up before we go to chapel.'

'Who's preaching tonight, Mam?' Mona asked.

'It's the Rev. Arthur Forrester. Not a preacher like Mr Featherstonhaugh – give a man a dog-collar and a living and it allus takes summat out of him. Still, he'll do. He's not a bad speaker.'

'Did you see me mam?' Joby asked.

'Aye.'

'How is she?'

'As well as can be expected, I reckon.'

'Did she read me letter?'

'Aye, and she sent you one back.' Aunt Daisy turned an accusing gaze on Joby. 'Why didn't you say you'd been up to the hospital last night? Why didn't you tell us when we asked you where you'd been?'

'I don't know.'

102

'You knew we'd get to know when you put it in that letter to your mam, didn't you?'

'I suppose so.'

' "I suppose so," ' Aunt Daisy mimicked. 'Sly, underhand ways. I don't know where you've learned behaviour like that, but I'll tell you this: there's no room for it in this house.'

'Can I have me mam's letter?'

'Have you never learned to say please, neither?'

'Please,' Joby said.

'That's more like it. Get him the letter out o' me handbag, Mona. I don't think he deserves it but I promised I'd give it to him.'

Joby tore open the envelope and took out the letter.

'Dear Joby, Thank you for writing me a letter and telling me what you've been up to. After all your Auntie Daisy's done you could have told her as well. I'm very cross with you for coming up here when you know little boys aren't allowed in and you are a very naughty boy for worrying your auntie after all she's done.

'So just mend your ways and show your auntie what a good lad you really are till I come home. I'm feeling quite well and I hope they'll soon tell me when I can come home. Love from Mam.'

7

Joby didn't see Snap for some time. He was glad in a way because he wouldn't have known what to say to him. It was usually Snap who called for Joby and now Joby waited for him to make the first move. There was a paragraph about Snap's uncle in Monday morning's *Yorkshire Post* and even a couple of lines in some of the national dailies. Later in the week some of them reported the inquest. There was no note. The coroner said it was tragic that an intelligent man like Snap's uncle, young and in the prime of life, spoken well of by all who knew him, should have killed himself. There was no record of illness or mental disease and no evidence of personal trouble, though his sister, Snap's mother, did say there had been times when he seemed rather depressed but she had put this down to the world situation which he felt strongly about. It was recorded that he had taken his life while the balance of his mind was disturbed.

Joby found himself more and more in the company of Gus and Tommy. Sometimes there were others of Gus's gang with them but more often it was the three of them who hung about together. There was, Joby found, something very engaging about Gus and you had to be his ally to appreciate it. For when you were on Gus's side you shared his glee in the tricks he got up to. There were some boys who were always fighting, but Gus wasn't one of them. He rarely fought, Joby found, but could command respect without it. He drew other boys to him without apparent effort. There were many who disliked him but most of them would have liked to be friendly with him. Like Joby himself. He had always thought he disliked Gus but now he found he didn't; and the difference was that he was on Gus's side. Being an intimate of Gus's gave Joby a very pleasant feeling of importance and he felt that other boys looked at him with increased respect. It was true that you never quite knew where you had Gus; there was something in him you could never quite be sure of; but he was great fun to be with.

Gus knew all the orchards worth scrumping and they raided them for hard green apples which they threw away half-eaten. They fished for newts in Gibbert's Dyke, climbed trees in the woods, kicked an old football about in the recreation ground, traversed the ironwork of the railway bridge over the river and dropped stones into the black greasy depths below. They conducted their first experiments in smoking with the aid of a machine which dispensed a packet containing two Woodbines and two matches for a penny. Or at least, Joby experimented, for it seemed that Gus was already an accomplished smoker who could tackle a cigarette in grown-man fashion without turning a hair. And then Gus and Tommy introduced Joby to an activity so exciting it galvanized him with a tension that seemed to charge his blood with electricity.

Tommy had a doctor's prescription to get filled for his father. Mr Masterman was a semi-invalid and needed a constant supply of pills and medicine. They took the prescription to a small shop where there was only the chemist himself and no assistant. He went into the back room with the slip of paper, leaving the three of them standing among the showcases of scent and soap and patent medicines, and the counter displays of shampoos, shaving soaps, cough pastilles, barley sugar lozenges, diabetics' chocolate and herbal cigarettes. The chemist had no sooner left them alone than Gus and Tommy began to help themselves, pocketing articles from the boxes on the counter. Joby stared in astonishment and terror. He felt like crying out to them to stop; then he wanted desperately to run away from this sudden awful danger. But he couldn't move. He had to stay there watching Gus and Tommy, though he was sure his face would betray them to the man when he came back. The door handle rattled and Joby's whole body seemed to give a violent twitch of fright. He turned away as someone came into the shop and looked with concentration at a presentation box of perfume in fancy bottles in a showcase on the wall. In a moment he forced himself to walk to the door without looking at anyone, open it and step outside.

He loitered by the window. His legs seemed to be directly connected to his feeling of fear. Ought he to let them have their way, let them carry him as fast as they could away from here? He walked a few nervous paces up the road and when he tried to turn again his legs refused to carry him back. The thought of what might be happening in the shop danced agitatedly in his mind. Suppose Gus and Tommy had been caught; would the chemist come out to look for him, the third member of the party? Well, he had nothing in his pockets for him to find. Yet he could be an accomplice, set to watch the door while they did the actual stealing.

He saw the door handle move and stood very still, watching it. He supposed it was no use running away now, but he wanted to so badly. His skin seemed alive with the tension of standing there as the door opened.

It swung right back. Gus and Tommy came out of the shop. Tommy closed the door behind them. He was carrying a box of pills and holding a paper-wrapped bottle of medicine against his chest with one arm. They walked towards him and Gus grinned. At once relief flooded through Joby, leaving him limp. His legs, with the tension gone from them, trembled slackly now as though they wouldn't hold him up.

'What did you buzz off out for?' Gus asked, the laughter mocking in his eyes.

'I thought you were gunna get caught any minute,' Joby said. 'Why didn't you tell me before we went in?'

'Mebbe you wouldn't ha' come in with us if you'd known,' Gus said. 'Now you know how easy it is. Were you scared?'

'Yeh, I was,' Joby admitted.

'Well, that's part of the fun. Come on, we don't want to hang about here. You take that stuff home for your old feller, Tommy, then we'll go somewhere an' look what we've got.'

'Do you do this a lot?' Joby asked.

'We know one or two places,' Gus said. 'Don't we, Tommy?'

'Aye, one or two,' Tommy said.

'Some places the crafty sods have mirrors so's they can see into the shop from the back,' Gus said. 'You've got to watch out for them.'

'An' you've never been copped?'

'Naw, we don't take risks, see.'

When they had delivered the medicine to Tommy's house they went into a corner of a field and examined their loot. Tommy even had a small bottle of scent.

'What you gunna do with that?' Gus asked him.

'I dunno,' Tommy shrugged.

'Why'd you pinch it, then?'

'I just picked it up.'

'You only wanna take stuff you can use,' Gus said, which Joby thought was a bit of a laugh because there was hardly anything they had got which seemed useful. Nothing, anyway, worth the risk of being caught.

'Mebbe I'll chuck it away,' Tommy said, holding the bottle up and watching the sunlight strike through the yellow glass. He unscrewed the cap and sniffed at the scent.

'Pooh, what a niff!'

'Whyn't you give it to Joby for his girl friend?'

'What girl friend?' Joby said, startled.

'Elsa Laedeker,' Gus said blandly. 'You're sweet on her, aren't you?'

'Who's been telling you a tale like that?'

'Oh, I dunno. I just thought you fancied her, that's all.'

'What if I do like her, anyway?'

'Nowt.'

'I've never even talked to her.'

'You wanna give her a present, man. A little bottle o' scent, or summat like that.'

'How can I when I don't talk to her?'

'Aw, you can allus manage to talk to her if you want to.'

Tommy held out the bottle to Joby.

'Want it, then?'

Joby hesitated, then took the bottle. 'Might as well, if you don't want it.' He put it in his pocket. He could always hide it somwhere. It struck him now that he really was an accomplice. But he didn't care.

Gus was lighting a herbal cigarette with a cardboard tip. He took a puff and pulled a face.

'Ugh, rammy. Want one, Joby?'

Joby said no. There was a thrill in smoking but it turned him dizzy and made him feel sick.

'Have a cough spice, then.'

'No, but I'll have a barley sugar.'

Gus tossed the packet across. 'Here, help yourself.' He lay on his back in the grass and puffed at the cigarette. 'Mmm, I reckon you can get used to 'em. Anyway, they didn't cost owt, did they?'

The droll way Gus came out with this started them all laughing. The laughter itself was infectious, as though they were confined in the classroom and not supposed to laugh at all. They lay in the grass and let it burst out of them till their eyes were full of tears and the laughter became a pain under their ribs. And with it began Joby's adjustment to a new way of thinking. The next time Gus and Tommy helped themselves in a shop he was a willing accomplice. In the process of vague reasoning through which his mind travelled he saw it all as a great lark. The loss of what they took wouldn't hurt anybody but to take it was to score points in the running battle between them and the world of grown-ups. The words 'dishonest', 'stealing' and 'thief' bounced off his conscience as descriptive of many people but not himself. The thing he could not get over was being scared, his nerves stretched taut and quivering with tension, but he learned to accept it as part of the game.

It was the most exciting game he had ever played. He didn't know how often Gus and Tommy had done it before but now it reached the intensity of a craze. They assessed the possibilities of every shop they went into and before long Joby became bold enough to do little jobs while he was alone. As a novelty they one day decided to take a look at Woolworths in Cressley, but after walking round they concluded that it was too risky with so many attendants and customers about and, for all they knew, somebody watching through peepholes high in the walls.

All this time Joby was watching for Elsa. He didn't know how he would start talking to her or what he would say, let alone give her the scent; but he kept on looking out for her. Sometimes when they had nothing special to do he and Gus and Tommy hung about at the end of Elsa's street, thinking they might see her in that way. But they saw her only once, when Mr Laedeker's car came along the main road; and then they had only just recognised it and realised that Elsa was sitting in front beside her father before it was past, bouncing gently away up the unmade road to the house. And Elsa had never even turned her head to glance at the three boys standing there. Why should she? How did they touch upon her cosy world; what part did they play in the scheme of home and school and friends and holidays? They stopped waiting after this. Gus and Tommy had humoured Joby so far but since they weren't interested in Elsa they thought it a useless and boring pastime. And Joby didn't feel able to hang about alone because of appearing foolish and conspicuous.

His mother came home. She had been away three weeks and they seemed like three months to Joby. She had orders to take things easy for a time but the doctors were apparently pleased with the success of her operation, which had not been as serious as everyone had thought it was going to be. Joby picked all this up from overheard scraps of conversation between his mother and the neighbours. She looked no different to him. She moved very steadily about the house and held herself a little stiffly about the left shoulder because she didn't want to disturb the freshly healed wound; but as far as he could tell she had come home whole and would not have to resort to the measure of Gus's aunt. Home enveloped Joby once more. He slept in his own bed and ate his meals with his mother. His father was quiet but Joby could tell he was happy that the family was whole again. In a few days it was as though his mother had never been away.

Snap finally turned up. He knocked at the back door while Joby was in the middle of his dinner.

'If it's a mate of yours don't stand all day talking to him while your dinner goes cold,' his mother said.

Joby opened the door and looked at Snap scraping

111

about in the dust of the yard with the end of his stick.

'Oh, hello, Snap.'

'Hi, Joby. How you doing?'

'Oh, okay.'

'Are you coming out this aft.?'

'I've fixed up to go out with Gus and Tommy.'

'Where to?'

'I dunno yet.'

'Are you knocking about with them now?'

'Yeh, I have been a bit . . . I heard about your uncle.'

'Yeh,' Snap said.

'I'm having me dinner. Me mam'll be mad if I don't go back in and finish.'

'Okay.'

'I reckon it'll be okay if you want to come with us.'

Snap shook his head. 'Naw, I don't like Gus Wilson.'

'He's okay when you get to know him.'

'Well, he doesn't like me, anyway.'

This was true. Gus was contemptuous of Snap and wouldn't welcome him into the gang. It was better too if Snap didn't find out what they were up to because somehow Joby didn't think he would want to join in that even if he were invited. Joby felt a small twinge of conscience and for a moment he was tempted to tell Snap to wait and he would go out with him this afternoon. Then his mother called out from inside the house and Snap began to mooch off along the yard.

'I'll see you some other time, then,' Snap said, and Joby called after him, 'Yeh, okay, Snap. See yer!'

'Who was it?' his mother asked.

'Snap.'

'What did *he* want?'

'He came to see if I was doing anything.'

'Are you going out with him?'

'No, I don't knock about with him now.'

'I should think not, either. I allus said there was summat not quite right about him. Now it strikes me it runs in the family. That uncle of his . . .'

'Oh, Snap's all right. I just haven't seen him lately.'

'I think you're better off without him.'

Joby didn't answer. He had never understood his mother's unreasonable dislike of Snap and it had often distressed him. You wanted all the people you loved or liked to like one another; but it seemed the world wasn't made like that. But now, in a curious way, his mother's opinion of Snap reassured him, armed him against the tiny pang of conscience that touched him again as he recalled Snap going away alone. It was almost as though Snap, in a way, *was* his conscience, standing behind him disapprovingly as he went off with Gus and Tommy. No, he couldn't have taken Snap along; he would never have fitted in or understood about the game. But what did he care about Snap, of all people? Had Snap spoken up for him when he was thrown out of the pictures? And what had happened when he had squared up to fight Gus? Snap had disappeared, run off. That was the kind of friend he was. He was, as his mother said, better off without him.

8

Joby sat at the table with a writing-pad, a pen and a bottle of ink. He had thought for a long time about the letter he was writing before sitting down to write it and what he had arrived at seemed to him the best he could do in the circumstances.

'Dear Elsa,' (he had wondered whether 'Miss Laedeker' mightn't be more correct, then decided it was altogether too stiff and starchy), 'I hope you will accept this small present from an admirer and that you will not think me too cheeky for writing to you. As I do not know you to speak to I could not think of any other way. I think you do not know me at all but if you would like to you can send me a message the way you got this. Yours sincerely, Joby Weston.'

Joby read what he had written and nodded with satisfaction. Say what you like, he knew how to write a letter. He didn't think anybody, including Snap, could have done any better. He wrote 'Miss E. Laedeker' on the outside of the envelope and put the letter and the phial of perfume inside. Then he took the writing-pad and pen and ink and put them away in the drawer before his mother came back from the shop.

It was Gus who had come up with the idea.

'I've just found out a lass I know called Joan Birch goes to play with Elsa Laedeker at their house.'

'What about it, then?'

'Well, you can send a letter to her, man, and the scent as well if you want. Then you might get to know her.'

The more Joby thought about it the more excited he became. It was a great idea.

'If I write a letter will you give it to this Joan Birch?'

"Course,' Gus said. 'You leave it to me.'

'An' you'll tell her to keep her mouth shut?' Joby said. 'I don't want her blabbin' it all over the place.'

'Don't worry,' Gus said, 'I'll see to it.'

The letter went on its way that afternoon. Gus took it with a conspiratorial wink and Joby felt a vague sense of apprehension as the envelope disappeared into Gus's pocket.

The feeling grew, especially after he had left Gus, and by the time he saw him the next day he was ready to ask for the letter back and call it all off. But Gus had already passed it to Joan and Elsa would probably get it sometime today. Now that the matter was out of his hands Joby was restless and uneasy. He could imagine Elsa and Joan giggling over his cheek in sending the letter and the scent and telling their friends and pointing him out on the street for all to laugh at. In fact, the more he thought about it the more he began to feel that he might have been mistaken altogether in the idea of affection for Elsa, and that he didn't really care for her one way or the other. What did he want with girls? He felt exposed now and wished frankly that Gus

115

had never had the idea. All he could do now, though, was wait and see what happened.

An old tennis ball bulged Gus's pocket. He took it out and they wandered aimlessly through the back streets near the church, tossing it to each other along the pavement. They were on their own and had been for the last couple of days. It was the town's holiday week and most of their friends were away at Blackpool or Morecambe or Bridlington. Their parents had saved all year through the various holiday clubs and now they would be splashing the lot on one glorious week away from work and cleaning and cooking. There would be Reginald Dixon at the organ of the Tower Ballroom, Blackpool, George Formby at the Palace Theatre and Albert Modley and Dave Morris on the piers. The strings of lights would be going up for the illuminations, and the open trams hooting down the promenade. There would be the Laughing Man and the Big Dipper on the Pleasure Beach, bags of piping-hot fish and chips, and picture postcards with enormously fat ladies in red bathing costumes, along the front; deck chairs and buckets and spades and sand-castles on the crowded beach. Rowing boats on the lake in Stanley Park and a military band playing selections from 'Merrie England', 'The Quaker Girl' and 'The Gondoliers'. Stomach-plunging ascents of the Tower where you could buy, write and post cards to those unfortunately not there and look through the rails at the Dinky cars running up and down the prom. Lancashire and Yorkshire voices everywhere, with a smattering of Welsh, Scots and Geordie, all laughing and shouting. Gangs of mill-girls arm-in-arm as they

116

straddled the pavements and threw out the challenge of their bright eyes and the messages on their paper hats: 'come and get me', 'oh, baby' and 'kiss me quick'.

Joby's parents had cancelled their holiday this year because of Joby's mother having to go into hospital. There had been some talk of her having a couple of weeks in a convalescent home, paid for out of the funds of Weston's sick club; but she had resisted this on the grounds that she couldn't leave her family and the house for another fortnight while she queened it at the sea-side. Perhaps they would manage a week-end in October when the illuminations were on, Weston said. But October was an age away and it seemed to Joby that all kinds of things might happen to spoil that plan. He also had an idea that money might be a bit scarce. There was some expense entailed in sending him to the grammar school. He would need a uniform and sports kit and a schoolbag. He was hoping finally to persuade his mother and father to buy him a bike to travel on every day (when his mother got over her fear of him riding on the roads) and this would be an economy in the long run, saving bus fares, but another initial expense to be met. Joby supposed he was lucky he was being allowed to go to grammar school. He knew boys who had passed the scholarship exam. and then been refused permission to go because their parents wanted them to start work at fourteen and bring some money into the house. And he recalled Audrey Adams, who was top of the class in everything, weeping in a corner because her parents didn't believe in the waste of educating a girl any further than they were compelled to. So really he could not grumble at missing his

117

holiday by the sea, though he couldn't help regretting it.

Joby threw the ball carelessly high. Gus leaped up, arm outstretched, to intercept it but it soared six inches above his hand and narrowly missed the peaked cap of the man pedalling the 'stop me and buy one' ice-cream tricycle across the junction. Gus darted across the road to recover the ball as it bounced by the window of a corner general shop. He was looking into the window when Joby came up to him and he turned his head with a sly sidelong grin that started Joby's pulse fluttering.

'Got any gelt?'

Joby dipped into the pocket of his shorts.

'Threepence-ha'penny. Haven't you got owt?'

Gus shook his head. 'Not a cent . . . What can we ask for that in't much?'

'Chewing gum?'

'Aye, that's it.'

Gus looked Joby full in the face and his grin broadened. Joby wondered what his own expression was like. Gus never looked scared, though he admitted to being so at times.

'Have you been in this one afore?'

'No, but it'll be okay. Want me to ask?'

'Yeh, you ask.'

He put two pennies into Gus's hand and Gus opened the door, setting a bell jangling. The inside of the shop was quiet and cool. There were jars of jam and lemon cheese, and cans of all kinds of things piled high on the shelves against the wall; boxes of sweets and custard powders on the L-shaped counter and an open sack of potatoes and another of sugar on the floor. They listened for someone coming but there was no sound from anywhere.

When Gus dipped his hand into a box of toffees it was like a signal to Joby. He followed suit while Gus, cool as you please, stretched himself right over the width of the counter to reach the cigarettes. At the back of Joby's mind as he stuffed handfuls of sweets into his pockets was the thought that the shopkeeper was a very long time in coming.

And just then the voice, like a kick to the heart, said, 'And what d'you think you're doing?'

They sprang round, their bodies stiffening into motionless attitudes of flight as they saw that the man was on their side of the counter, between them and the door. Shock robbed them of their voices. They gaped at him, saying nothing. The shopkeeper, a thin elderly man in a khaki smock, reached out and slid the bolt on the door, cutting off all hope of escape.

'I asked you what you thought you were doing.'

His voice was stiff and cold as iron. Joby, weak with shock and fright, thought he had never heard a voice like it, nor a face so hard and ungiving as this man's. Oh! but he had dreaded this from the first. He had known it must happen some time. If only they could go back ten minutes and be playing with the ball in the street and no thought of the shop in their heads!

Gus managed to speak. 'We wanted some chewing gum, please,' he said, as though he didn't understand the man.

'Yes, that's right,' Joby heard himself babbling. 'Just some chewing gum. He's got the money for it.' He gestured towards Gus who opened his hand and showed the two pennies in his palm.

'Chewing gum, eh? Well, you won't find any in that box o' toffees, nor under the counter, either.'

He squared his thin shoulders inside the khaki smock. His bushy grey eyebrows frothed over the rims of his spectacles and his eyes were bright and hard as he looked at them. He waved his hand towards the rear premises.

'You'd better go through there wi' me. Go on, now, let's be having you!'

He ushered them before him into the living-room. They stood near the table, not knowing what to do with their hands.

'Are you going to fetch a bobby?' Joby asked.

A swift kaleidoscopic view of the sequence of disgrace flashed through his mind. The police at home; the surprise and shame of his parents; everybody knowing; the scene in court; grammar school barred to him because he was a bad character; probably Borstal instead, or somewhere just as bad. He wanted to sit down. The fear was in his legs and they wouldn't hold him up much longer.

The shopkeeper ignored the question. He said, 'Now then, empty your pockets.'

Eagerly Joby put toffees on the table, searching carefully for any lurking in the corners of his pockets. Gus produced two ten packets of Woodbines in addition to sweets. To these they added the miscellaneous bits and pieces of useful junk which their pockets collected.

The shopkeeper looked at it. 'Is that all?'

They nodded together. The man pushed his own property to one side then took off his glasses and rubbed his eyelids with his free hand. Joby wanted to exchange a quick look with Gus and receive some signal of reassurance; but he could only shoot frightened little glances at the face of the shopkeeper. He hastily averted his eyes as the man lifted his head and replaced his spectacles.

'What's your name?' he asked Gus. 'Your real one, mind.'

Gus told him and the man nodded as though he knew all about him. 'And who might you be?' he said to Joby.

'Joseph Weston,' Joby said. 'Everybody calls me Joby.'

'What would you think to everybody calling you "thief"?' the man shot at him.

'I wouldn't like it,' Joby mumbled.

'No . . . Well, you'd better tell me what made you come into my shop to steal. How long have you been doing this kind o' thing? D'you make a practice of it in every shop you go into?'

Gus answered him and he sounded desperately earnest and sincere.

'No, we're not thieves, Mister, honest. We just thought it'd be a bit o' fun. It was a sort o' dare like, y'know. We were a bit fed-up with all our mates off on their holidays an' that. We'd never do it again, would we, Joby? This has learned us a lesson.'

'Fun, eh? You know where that kind o' fun'll land you, don't you? Into reform school. And there's no home comforts there, nor holidays at the sea-side

121

neither. And when you get out everybody 'ull know you for convicted thieves and nobody 'ull trust you any more. What sort of a start in life is that? You might think you've all the time in the world but you'll be thinking about earning a living afore you know it and you won't get far without a clean sheet . . . What school do you go to?'

'Tinsley Road,' Gus said.

'I'm going to Cressley Grammar School in September,' Joby said.

'Did you pass your scholarship?' The man looked at Joby as he nodded. 'Then why the hangman do you want to spoil such a chance by carrying on like this?'

It was the tone of weary exasperation in which he spoke now that made Joby realise he was not going to report what had happened. He hardly heard the rest of what was said through the light-headed feeling of his relief.

'Pick your tackle up and get off home.' The shop-keeper moved away from the fireplace. 'And have a good think about what I've told you.'

They scraped their belongings into their pockets and made for the door.

'You can go out the back way,' the man said and opened the door and stood aside to let them pass.

'Are you going to tell us dads?' Gus said.

'You'd better wait and see about that. But remember this, I know who you are and if I hear tell of you getting into any more scrapes like this Is'll go straight to the police and tell 'em about today.'

'Don't worry, Mister,' Gus said fervently, 'we shan't get into trouble again. We've had enough today.'

He stepped out into the yard. Behind him Joby hesitated. He wanted to say something. He felt he should. There was in him a sense of release as though a great load had been lifted from him.

He looked up at the man and said, 'Thanks, Mister. Thanks very much.'

The shopkeeper put his hand on Joby's shoulder and pushed him out after Gus. 'Get off home. Just think on what I've told you an' you'll be all right.'

They didn't speak until they had gone some way from the shop, then Gus said, 'Crikey, I thought we were in for it that time!'

'Me an' all.' Joby looked sideways at Gus's face, trying to read his expression. 'I reckon we'd better stop it now,' he said.

'Aye, we'd better. It's not safe now.'

They went into a field and sat down to talk about what had happened. Wisps of fear still troubled Joby now that he was away from the shop.

'D'you think he will tell us dads?' he said.

Gus was confident. 'Naw, he won't tell now. He let us off with a good talking-to, didn't he?'

The church clock struck the half hour.

'What time's that, then?'

'Half-past four.'

'Is'll have to be off home for me tea,' Joby said.

'Aw, there's plenty o' time.' Gus sat up and looked all round the empty meadow. 'What about havin' a quick drag first?' He put his hand into his pocket and brought out a new packet of Woodbines. Joby stared at it.

'Where'd you get them?'

123

Gus grinned. 'Where d'you think?'

'But you give 'em all back.'

'All except these.'

A grin of mingled admiration and unease forced itself on to Joby's face.

'Honest, Gus, you're the blinkin' limit.'

'Well, are we gunna light up, then?' Gus said.

'No.' Joby scrambled to his feet. 'I've got to go. Me mam said I hadn't got to be late. I'll see you later. So long.'

He began to walk away across the rough grass. By the time he reached the boundary fence he was running. He wondered what Gus thought of him and didn't care. His only concern now was to get as far away from Gus as possible.

9

'An' then – you'll never credit it – he came to right in the middle of his operation and there was all his stomach laid out on the table at side of him. They'd never put him out properly, y'see.'

Mrs Collins, their next-door neighbour, was telling the amazing story of a relative of hers with a bland ghoulishness that froze Joby's blood. He listened, awe-struck.

'Heavens above!' Joby's mother said. 'And whatever happened then?'

'Well, he just laid there ever so quiet for a minute or two, watching what they were doing like. An' then one of 'em spotted he was wide awake and give him another whiff of the ether, right sharp.'

'I should just think so,' Joby's mother said.

'O' course, Frank had a professional interest in it like, him havin' been a first-aid man nearly all his married life, an' he said after he wished they'd left him alone so's he could watch a bit longer. He said they didn't half make a fuss of him after, trying to pass it over, y'see, so's he wouldn't lodge any complaints, him knowing the ropes an' all that . . . There's a lot goes on in them places 'at nobody outside ever gets to know about, y'know. When all's said an' done, you put your life in their hands an' if they make a mistake there's nowt you can do about it because they all stick up for one another. As thick as thieves, they are, in hospitals.'

'I must say they did well for me in the General,' Joby's mother said.

'Ah well, it wasn't as bad as they thought, was it? It's when you get complications 'at trouble starts. Like when I had our Walter. By, but he caused some trouble getting here, that lad! Blood? You've never seen so much. That delivery room was just like a slaughter-house. For all the world as if they'd been killing a beast.'

'Aren't you going out to play, Joby?' his mother said.

'In a minute,' Joby said. 'I'm just finishing me comic.'

'Aye, what a do that was,' Mrs Collins said. 'An' then when I had our Margaret it was as different again: as easy as shelling peas.' She shook her head reflectively. 'You never can tell. And that reminds me – have you heard about that Macleod lass up the street?'

'No, what about her?'

'They say she's havin' a bairn . . .'

Out of the top of his vision Joby saw the quick lift of his mother's hand and the inclination of her head in his direction.

'Joby, off you go out and play while the sun's still shining.'

He got up. He was only too glad to go now. His cheeks, after the initial heart-stopping shock, were burning.

126

'It's all up and down the street,' Mrs Collins said, too eager to impart her gossip to wait till he was gone. He lingered for a moment on the back step. 'I allus knew she'd get herself into a mess afore she'd done.'

Joby's mouth was dry as he walked away down the yard. A baby! He wondered if they knew who was responsible and his immediate thought was to get away from the house before his mother by some instinct realised the truth and called him back. He remembered Mollie's wanton laugh in the field, her skirt up round her waist, and her bright eyes as she egged him on. He broke into a run through the entry, his shoes clattering on the brick paving.

Emerging into the street he reached up in an instinctive movement and grabbed a ball out of the air. He threw it back to the group of big lads playing thirty yards away. A good catch. He would never have managed it if he'd had time to think about it. A little feat like that would normally make you feel good for some time. But now . . .

A black car was creeping up the street, close in to the kerb. The driver seemed to be peering at each house as he passed. He stopped before Joby reached him and spoke through the open window. It was when he spoke that Joby realised who the man was, though he had never heard his voice before.

'Young man, can you tell me where the Westons live, please?'

The accent was pronounced but did not spoil the clarity of the English.

It was not in Joby's nature to bluff for nothing. If he

said the wrong house the occupants would put the visitor right and wonder who he was afterwards.

'Number twenty-nine. Up there on the right-hand side.'

'Thank you very much.'

Joby made off before the man could ask him anything else. At the corner he stopped and watched the car come to a halt outside their house. Mr Laedeker got out and stepped across the pavement to the front door. He lifted his hand to knock.

Joby ran. If only, his mind said over and over again to the rhythm of his feet. He had thought himself full of worry and care when his mother was in hospital but now the consequences of his misdeeds were falling on him thick and fast. If only he had not gone for that walk with Mollie; if only he hadn't chummed up with Gus and Tommy and allowed Tommy to give him the scent. If only, even then, he hadn't listened to Gus's idea about sending the present to Elsa. Elsa? He couldn't conceive now how he had ever thought of her as someone special. And if he thought about the rest of it, well all that hinged upon his being thrown out of the pictures. If that hadn't happened he wouldn't have met Mollie, nor fought with Gus, nor got himself into the mood that sent him up to the hospital and led to his skipping Sunday School next day. The thought of that little elderly attendant exercising his authority on the wrong boy filled Joby with impotent fury. That had started it all. Of course, he'd no need to have done all the other things, had he? No, but still . . .

He went down to Snap's but the house was locked up and quiet, everybody out. He thought that Snap

128

must have gone off somewhere with his mother, it being Saturday. He hadn't really wanted to see Snap or anybody else, but there were one or two points he thought Snap might have been able to clear up for him, though he would have had to put them in a roundabout way. Now there was nothing for him to do but go back and face the music. He could stay out till tea-time but it would still be the same and it might give his mother time to get worked up about it all. At least its happening today meant he hadn't his dad to face straight away as well because he had gone off to Rochdale to see Joby's uncle who was apparently ill. Somebody had rung up the works yesterday to tell his dad and he had taken Saturday morning off and gone first thing. Joby's mother had wanted Weston to take Joby with him for the trip but Weston had said no, he didn't know how bad Clifford was and they mightn't want kids cluttering up the place at such a time. And Joby, who detested his cousin Hector, had not complained.

He was grateful to notice, when he got into the street, that the car had gone. He wandered slowly along, trailing his hand along the walls, wondering what he was going to say to his mother and coming to the realisation that he didn't know exactly what she would know and until she told him he couldn't plan any story. He was half-way up the street when Mollie Macleod ran out of their entry as though nothing at all was wrong with her. She shouted to him.

'Ey, Joby, what you doing?'

'Just going in home,' Joby said. He stared at her as she came closer. She was laughing openly.

'Looks as though there'll be no more tanners from our lass,' she said.

'Why, what's up?'

'There's nowt to tell on her about now . . . Haven't you heard?' Mollie hugged herself with glee. 'The big daft devil's gone and got herself into trouble. She's having a kid.'

'You mean your Agnes?' Joby said.

'Hadn't you heard?'

'Well, I did hear summat . . .'

'It's our kid,' Mollie said. 'You didn't think it was me, did you?' She saw the colour in his cheeks and laughed out loud. 'Honest, Joby, you are a duck-egg.'

Yes, he was. How was it he never seemed to know anything about anything?

'You an' me couldn't make a kid,' Mollie said. 'Anyway, we didn't do anything to make one. And if we had we wouldn't know yet.'

'You don't have to tell me,' Joby said. 'I'm not daft.'

He turned and walked away from Mollie. She called after him:

'You ask your mam to tell you all about it.'

He felt foolish but he didn't really mind that. It was one problem solved. He only needed to know now what Mr Laedeker had called about.

His mother didn't need to speak when he went into the house. The evidence was on the table.

'Come in, you,' his mother said. Mrs Collins had gone and she was alone. 'I want to talk to you.'

'Oh? What about?'

'Have you seen that before?' She pointed to the small yellow phial of perfume standing in the centre of the green tablecloth.

'What is it?'

'You can see what it is. I want to know if you've seen it before.'

Joby cleared his throat. 'I might have.'

'Oh, you might have. And how might you have?'

'I don't know what you're getting at,' Joby said.

'Well happen this'll make it plainer.' She took from her apron pocket a sheet of paper which she opened and placed on the table. It was the letter he had so carefully composed for Elsa.

'Is that your writing?'

Well, he couldn't deny that. He was sunk. He nodded.

'Love letters to lasses at your age,' his mother said.

'It's not a love letter,' Joby said. 'There's no love in it.'

'We won't argue about that. What I'm bothered about is that bottle o' scent.'

'Have you had somebody to see you?'

'Yes, I've had Mr Laedeker. He's a very nice man. When his daughter receives expensive presents from strange boys he likes to know what it's all about.'

'It wasn't expensive.'

'How much was it, then?'

Joby hesitated for a fraction of a second. 'Half a crown.'

'Not quick enough, lad. And not true, either. Mr Laedeker took the trouble to find out about it and he says a bottle of perfume like that costs eleven and sixpence in a chemist's shop. Now, where did you get eleven and sixpence from to buy it?'

'I didn't buy it . . . I had it given.'

'Well, that's a likely story, anyway. Now, I'm warning you, young man, I'm in the mood to give you a good hiding, so you'd better make up your mind to tell me the truth.'

'It is the truth,' Joby said. 'Another lad gave it to me.'

'Who was he?'

'I can't tell.'

'You mean you won't tell. How do you expect me to believe you if you won't tell me who he is?'

'I can't split on him, Mam,' Joby said.

'Did this lad steal the scent?'

Joby nodded. 'Yeh, I think so.'

'And yet you took it, knowing it to be stolen? Now, Joby, look me in the face and tell me the truth. Did you steal it yourself?'

Joby looked into his mother's face. He was bound to feel guilty knowing the occasions when he *had* been dishonest.

'I didn't pinch it.'

'Was it this mate of yours – Snap?'

'No, Snap's not like that.'

'Well, that's one point in his favour, anyway. I never knew you were like that before. I don't know what you've been up to while I've been away . . . You deserve a damn' good hiding and if your father was here he'd give you one. Anyway, you can get off to bed.'

'But it's only half-past three!'

'I know it is. But you're going upstairs all the same.

Happen you'll have time to think what sort of a lad you've turned into; and perhaps you'll think of a few more things you ought to tell me.'

She turned away from him and he saw that the tension had gone from her. She had given him many a sharp clout for everyday misdemeanours, but it seemed that this was too serious for that. She was upset and his heart yearned towards her. He was full of shame and he wanted badly to comfort her and assure her that it was all right, that he had learned his lesson; that, in a way, it had all happened because he was missing her so much and he couldn't reach anybody else. But there were not words for all that. He got up and made for the door to the stairs.

'I'm sorry, Mam,' he said.

'And so you should be,' she said over her shoulder. 'Now get off up and get undressed.'

'Can I read for a bit?'

'Oh, I reckon so. If you go to sleep now you'll never sleep tonight.'

Joby went upstairs. His room was cool, even slightly chilly, the sun having moved away from this side of the house during the morning. He undressed and put on his pyjamas and got into bed. There was a large pile of comics by the bed but after glancing through the top few he put them aside and reached down into the cupboard to his books. He found *Coral Island* and decided to read that again; but first he found the passages where the man was buried alive and the cannibals launched their canoes over the living bodies of their captives. These two sequences always made him feel sick and impressed upon him how fortunate he was. Most of the trouble in the world was caused by people. Joby wondered why it was. Somehow he thought the troublemakers were not all wicked; and even if they were they perhaps didn't know it. He thought that many of them must feel as he had when he was stealing: that the rules somehow didn't apply to him because he was himself and not other people, and he could steal without being a thief. Even now he felt no real shame for the acts themselves. What troubled him was the effect on his mother, who couldn't possibly be expected to see it from his point of view. It was this effect that made it all, for the first time, seem wrong.

The fact of being in bed made him feel drowsy after a time and he put the book down and snuggled under the bedclothes. He felt almost happy now at having shed the tensions of the past few weeks. If only he hadn't still to face his father . . . He fell asleep wondering if his mother would tell and woke to find that all the brightness had gone out of the sky. He knew by this that it must be late but he had no watch to tell the time by. Perhaps there would be a chance of his mother and dad buying him a watch when he started grammar school. It was unlikely, what with all the other expense, but you never knew. If he did his lessons well and got good marks during the first term they might be proud enough of him at Christmas to buy him a cheap one.

He was thirsty and also rather hungry. The thought of coming face to face with his father deterred him for some time from going down to ask his mother for supper; but then he got out of bed to carry out a reconnaissance.

As soon as he opened the bedroom door he heard voices in the living-room. He couldn't make out what was being said but the voices were lively and sounded like women's. He stole downstairs until he was standing in the draughty little passage outside the living-room door. He knew now that one of the women was Aunt Daisy and she sounded to be having a sharp exchange with his mother.

'Well, what do you expect me to say, Daisy, till I hear Reg's side of it? It's all very well you dragging our Mona round here by the scruff of the neck, but I reckon he'll have summat to say when he comes home.'

'*If* he comes home,' Aunt Daisy said. 'If you ask me he'll be too shamefaced to show himself round here for a bit. And quite right too. Anyway, you sound as if you don't believe what our Mona says.'

'I never said that. I reckon she knows what she says, but I'm wondering how many fanciful ideas she's got mixed up with it all.'

'What d'you mean "fanciful"? Hasn't she just said—'

'You know how she is.'

'No, I don't know. You'd better tell us while she's here to listen.'

'All right, then,' Joby's mother flared in exasperation. 'I mean she's bloody gormless enough to imagine owt. You know yourself she walks about in a waking dream, too flamin' silly to go t'last.'

'Oh, Auntie Norah!' Mona wailed.

'It's no good you Oh, Auntie Norahing me now. You should be old enough and sensible enough to know not to mess about with married men, wheedling

135

round 'em till they don't know whether they're coming or going!'

'Now just a minute, Norah; I'm not having that. Our Mona's allus been a straightforward lass, for all her faults. She's never had any trouble with men afore. You're not trying to tell me it was her idea to run off like that.'

'Happen not, but she wants a damn' good clout to brighten her ideas up.'

'And she's had one. She got one when she come home and told me what had happened. And she'll very likely get another when Ted hears about it.'

'Oh, I'm sorry, Mam, I'm sorry. I wish it had never happened.'

'You should ha' thought about that afore, instead o' bringing disgrace on us all. You know I'll never be able to hold me head up in t'street again. How d'you think I feel about it, eh? But I'm only your mother.'

'Happen you'll feel better about it if you don't blab it all over the place and try to make a martyr of yourself,' Joby's mother said.

'Why, Norah, I don't know how you can say such things.'

'I can say 'em because I know you, Daisy. You've been badly done to all your life, allus looking for slights where there isn't any and setting yourself up as a flamin' whited sepulchre, better than anybody else.'

'I've done nowt but try to live a clean an' upright life an' do me duty as I see it. An' the world 'ud be a sight better place if everybody else did the same.'

'It'd be a sorrier place for you with nobody to look down on an' condemn. I know you're upset over this, and you've every right to be; but you can't tell me there isn't a bit of you enjoying it.'

'Why, I've never heard such talk in my life. I don't know how you can—'

Joby, his bare feet almost frozen from standing in the passage, opened the door and walked into the living-room.

'And what are you doing out of bed, young man?'

He looked at them in the gathering dusk: Mona sitting with her head down, Aunt Daisy bolt upright on a straight chair, his mother standing on one side of the fireplace.

'I want some supper.'

'Well there is none.'

'Can I have a drink of water, then?'

His mother ran him a tumbler of water and gave it to him. Then she opened the cupboard and gave him two wholemeal biscuits.

'Here, take these up with you. An' don't make crumbs all over the bedclothes.'

'Has me dad come home yet?'

'No. He'll happen be here in the morning.'

Aunt Daisy snorted and Joby saw his mother's mouth tighten.

'Go on, off you go back to bed.'

'I'm not tired now.'

'It makes no difference. Go on, get off.'

'That poor bairn,' Aunt Daisy said.

'Oh, don't talk so soft, Daisy,' his mother said . . . 'Joby, did you hear me? I shan't tell you again.'

Joby went out of the room, pulling the door to behind him but not closing it. He stood in the passage again. His feet were still cold and he wished he'd thought to put on his stockings. But he hung on a little longer. He still couldn't make out what had happened; why his mother and Aunt Daisy were so cross with each other, and where Mona and his dad fitted in.

'You're a hard woman, Norah,' Aunt Daisy was saying.

'Me? Hard? I allus thought you were the hard one in the family, Daisy.'

'You must ha' been hard with Reg an' all, or he'd not have done what he has. Men don't do that sort o' thing without reason.'

'Oh, so I'm to blame for it now, am I?'

'You must have given him cause, Norah.'

'Cause? There's your cause, sitting there weeping like a bairn; her with her big bust and her bare legs and her simple ways. She's got no more sense than to go stirring a feller up, and too daft to know when she's doing it.'

'All I can say is you can't have been to him what you should have been.'

'Aye, and a damn' fine chance I've had this past few months, haven't I? And when I've gone through all that and come out of hospital what do I find? That me own niece has been making up to me husband while I was out of the way. Well it's a pity she didn't do it with some single young feller who'd get her in a field an' show her what's what.'

'You can't be sure your Reg hasn't shown her, can you?'

'Oh, Mam, I told you—'

'It's your own lass you're talking about, Daisy.'

138

'Aye, and your husband.'

'Well, we'd better get to know, then, while we're about it.'

'She says he hasn't hardly touched her.'

'I'd like to hear it for meself. Come on, Mona, out with it. How far have you gone with your Uncle Reg?'

Joby could hear that Mona was weeping. Her voice was wailing and full of tears.

'I've told me mam. He only kissed me. I wouldn't let him do anything else.'

'Did he try?'

'He touched . . . he touched me here, once or twice.'

'Did he put his hand inside your clothes?' Aunt Daisy said.

'No, I wouldn't let him. He wanted me to let him. He said I'd drive him mad. He said he loved me and wanted me to go away with him. I told him not to be so daft but he kept on trying to persuade me. He said we could go to Blackpool for a bit an' have a holiday and then he'd find another job and get a divorce so's we could get married.'

'My God!' Joby's mother said.

'Aye, you need say so, Norah. You need say so. That's right, go on, you shed a few tears now. I was wondering when you were going to.'

'And when we got to Manchester I got frightened,' Mona said, 'so I run off the train and let it go without me.'

'To think,' Joby's mother said, 'he had to make a fool of himself over a big soft lump like you.'

'If you're going to get nasty, Norah, we'd better go.'

'Aye, you better had. You're doing no good here.'

139

'Don't think you've heard the last of it, though.'

'The last of it? What the hell do you think you're talking about, Daisy? Me husband run off with a lass and now he's God knows where and you talk about not hearing the last of it.'

'We'll leave you on your own to think about it. You might think about offering up a little prayer while you're waiting. I've allus found it helps.'

'Oh, get off, and take your flamin' humbug with you.'

'I'm warning you, Norah. I've done my best to be fair and patient, but you're trying me too far.'

'Good night, Daisy.'

'I'll be round in the morning.'

'You've no need.'

'Ah, but I want to have a few words with Master Reg. If he comes back.'

There were sounds of movement towards the door. Joby ran as softly as he could upstairs, the water in the glass slopping over his hand and wrist. He had been so absorbed in what was being said he'd forgotten his thirst. In his bedroom he drank deeply from the glass and bit into one of the biscuits. He heard his Aunt Daisy and Mona leave and sat on the edge of his bed and thought about what he had heard. 'If he comes back,' Aunt Daisy had said. '*If* he comes back.'

It was almost dark now. He finished the biscuits and drank off the water then ran his tongue round his teeth, poking crumbs from between them. He heard no sound of his mother coming to bed and after a time he felt for his socks and put them on and went downstairs.

The living-room was in darkness but his eyes were

140

accustomed to the dusk and he could make out his mother sitting very still in an armchair by the empty fireplace.

'Don't you want a light on?'

'No. I don't want to look at anything.'

He took his hand away from the switch and moved a little farther into the room.

'Hasn't me dad come back yet?'

'No, not yet.'

'When will he come back?'

'Tomorrow, happen ... You'd better go back to bed.'

'Aren't you coming?'

'In a bit.'

He moved closer to her.

'Mam.'

'What?'

'I'm sorry, Mam. I mean about the scent an' all that.'

She said nothing and in a moment he went back to the door. He had the impression she was crying. But he couldn't be sure because of the dark, and she was making no sound.

10

The frail old lady with the shawl round her shoulders came out of the next house and looked at Joby standing on Snap's doorstep.

'It's no use knocking there, young man,' she said. 'They're all away. They've gone on their holidays to Bridlington.' Her voice was as light and insubstantial as her body.

'Have they gone for the week?' Joby asked.

'As far as I know, they have. Was it young Sidney you wanted?'

'Yes, it was.'

'Well, they've all gone; so you'll have to wait till they come back.'

'Yes, all right, then. I'll be off.'

'Just a minute, though.' The old lady moved her head up and down, peering at Joby alternately over the top of her glasses and through them. 'Are you in a hurry? Have you got to go somewhere?'

Joby shook his head and moved towards her across the double width of flagstones which ran along the fronts of the houses.

'What's your name?' the old lady asked him.

'Joseph Weston.'

'Have I seen you before?'

'I don't know. I've been here a few times.'

'Aye, I thought so. Do you go to school with Sidney?'

'I did till the end of last term; but I'm going to grammar school next month. I passed me scholarship.'

'Oh.' The old lady nodded several times. 'Oh. Well then, I wonder if you'd spare me a minute and come inside.'

The old lady turned and led the way into the house. The living-room, beautifully clean and neat, contained the faint but unmistakable odour of old age. The old lady crossed steadily to the mantelshelf and took down an envelope.

'This came through the post this morning,' she said, turning once more to Joby. 'It's from my eldest son; I can tell by the writing, how he makes his letters, y'know. I wonder, seeing that you're a scholarship boy, if you could read it to me.'

Joby wondered for a moment if she was giving him some kind of test and then it dawned on him that the old lady couldn't read.

'We never had much schooling when I was a lass,' she said, fumbling in the envelope with unsteady fingers and taking out a sheet of writing-paper. 'I don't suppose I had more than a twelve-month all told. It's different now. You young fowk have all the chances we never had.' She held out the letter and Joby took it. 'Here, see if you can fathom it.'

'It's from Coventry,' Joby said, glancing at the address.

'Aye,' the old lady nodded. That's where he lives.

He went down there three years ago to a job in a motor-factory. He helps to put all these motor cars together 'at you see on the roads.'

Joby was scanning the first page of the letter while the old lady was talking. He found that his hand was trembling.

'What's he got to say, then?'

'I . . . I can't really make it out,' Joby stammered. 'He doesn't write right plain, does he?'

'Oh? I allus thought he did: Mrs Prendergast says he's a very clear writer. She usually reads his letters to me an' then writes back for me. I don't like to ask the woman at the other side – Mrs Carter. She hasn't lived here long and I allus think she's a bit of a nosy parker.'

'I'm not right good with handwriting,' Joby said.

'Can't you make it out at all?'

Joby shook his head. His face was scarlet, he knew, but he didn't think the old lady's eyes were keen enough to notice it.

'Well, I thought you said you'd passed your scholarship. I shouldn't have thought you'd get very far at grammar school if you can't read a letter.'

'I'm better at some things than others,' Joby said. 'I'm good at history.'

'Ah well, I can't read a word, so I've nowt to talk about.' She took the letter back and put it away. 'Happen I'll get Mrs Carter to look at it for me in the morning.'

'That'll be best,' Joby said. 'I'm sorry.'

'Oh, it doesn't matter. There's nowt spoiling 'at I know of. It'll be just bits o' news about the family an' that. But he knows I like to know what's going on. He

144

doesn't get up here very often, y'see, it being so far to come. He says it'd be handy if he could borrow a car out of the works at week-ends. Just his joke, y'know. He's a great joker, is William. Allus full o' fun.'

'I'd better be going.' Joby said, making for the door.

'Aye, all right, then. And thank you for your trouble.'

'I wish I could have read it for you.'

'You did your best, I reckon.' The old lady followed him to the door. 'But I'd study at that, if I were you. You'll be handicapped if you can't read handwriting.'

'Yes, I know,' Joby said. 'Good night, then.'

The old lady gave him a farewell nod and stood to watch him go up the lane. He wondered if he had done the right thing and knew that he could not have brought himself to read out the first sentences of the letter: 'Dear Mother, I'm afraid this letter brings you bad news. You will be shocked to know that Cynthia was knocked down by a bus the day before yesterday and died in hospital last night. It was nobody's fault. She ran out of the house like kids do . . .'

His mother had gone about all day withdrawn into a silence so painful he had felt he must speak in whispers. She had said nothing to him in explanation of last night's visit of Aunt Daisy and Mona, and knowing as much as he did he asked no questions. Aunt Daisy appeared again after evening chapel, this time bringing Uncle Ted with her. He seemed very uneasy and came into the house with a red face and eyes that wouldn't settle on anything.

'Now then, Norah,' he said simply, in greeting.

'Now then, Ted.'

145

'It's a bit of a mess, taken all round, in't it?'

'Aye.'

Joby's mother was wearing her pride. Her eyes were not still either but she stood erect in the presence of her visitors.

'There's no sign or word of him yet, then?'

'No, not yet.'

'You don't think you happen ought to inform the police?'

'What for? It's no business of theirs. He's free to go as he pleases an' come back t'same way.'

'You can't just sit back an' take that attitude,' Aunt Daisy broke in.

'I can take whatever attitude I like,' Joby's mother said, and at this point Joby was sent out of the house.

The sun was going down beyond the great reefs of cloud which were full of orange-pink light. It would normally be time for him to be going in, but he didn't want to go back if Aunt Daisy and Uncle Ted were still there because his mother would only send him straight to bed out of the way. So he turned away from home and walked down the lane past the cricket field, kicking a stone before him at the peril of skinning the toes of his best brown shoes. A couple of mongrel dogs, one large, black and smooth-haired, the other smaller with a long black and white coat, frolicked on the edge of the field, running round and round, constantly exchanging the roles of pursuer and pursued, jumping at each other and sometimes rolling over and over together, ecstatic in each other's company. The smaller dog was often in the field and had sometimes attached itself to Joby and Snap, hopefully bringing sticks for

146

them to throw for it long after they were tired of the game. It had also, on occasion, made a nuisance of itself at cricket matches, streaking on to the field after the ball, causing fielders to fumble and some of the spectators to laugh. He had no idea whom the dog belonged to nor its name, but he called out to it now:

'Ey, boy! Here, boy! Come on now. Here, boy!'

The dog stopped its frolicking for a moment and looked in his direction, panting and open-mouthed. It seemed to grin in recognition. If it could have talked it might have said, 'See you another time; I've got a better game here.' For almost at once it spun away and hurled itself back into the fun with its big friend, which had taken advantage of the respite to cock up its leg against a tree.

Joby left them to it and walked on down past the council estate, thinking again of the old lady and her unread letter. She would learn the news in the morning when her neighbour saw the letter; but then she would not have to go straight to bed with it, all alone, with nobody to talk to. It would be easy now to feel proud that he had spared the old lady that, but he knew that his motives had been largely selfish. He had been scared stiff of witnessing the old lady's reaction to the bad news, of becoming involved in her shock and grief. Perhaps, he thought, she might have dropped straight down dead; though this was unlikely, for the tenacity of old people was a marvellous thing. Living alone, often with hardly any money, they took all kinds of disaster in their stride, showing an acceptance of life that was to be wondered at. And he thought that this might come from the knowledge that their own days

147

were numbered; a knowledge that his own mind couldn't conceive, just as he couldn't imagine that they had ever been as young as he was, or that one day he would be old, or even eighteen.

Twenty minutes later he was on the riverside and half way round the circle he had set out to cover from the town and back again. By the time he got home now the visitors would probably have gone and his father might have come back. But he had walked too far for his shoes, which weren't properly broken in, and the right one was rubbing a blister on his heel. He sat down on the grass and wondered whether he would be able to get the shoe back on if he took it off for a moment. It was getting late. Though the air was still warm the sun had gone and the flush of light had faded out of the clouds which seemed now to be dispersing into the pale grey of the sky. On his way Joby had passed several couples and one or two family groups returning from their Sunday-evening strolls; but now there was no one about except a solitary man sitting on the grass between the path and the river's edge some way off. Joby was on his feet again and limping towards the man before he realised who he was. His surprise was so great then that he stopped, feeling a sudden impulse to hide so that he wouldn't be seen. Then he went on again to where his father was stretched out on the grass, his weight on one elbow, looking into the river.

He didn't know whether his father had seen him coming or not but he glanced round without apparent surprise when Joby stopped some yards from him and said, 'Hello, Dad.'

148

'Hello, Joby,' Weston said dully. He resumed his contemplation of the river.

'What you doing here, Dad?' Joby asked.

He remained where he was, watching his father half lying there with his long legs stretched out towards the river, ankles crossed, one foot pointing skywards. He was wearing his best suit and a new cap. His heavy fingers played with a blade of grass, twirling it and twisting it, then finally letting it fall.

'I'm just sittin' and thinkin',' he said at last.

'What you thinking about?' Joby said.

'Oh . . . things. Things you don't understand.'

His best clothes somehow added to the strangeness of his sitting there alone like this, and as Joby looked at him he experienced for the first time a sense of his father as not his father, as someone without connection with himself; as a man, with thoughts and feelings outside their dual existence as father and son. He saw for the first time his father as a person carrying about with him a world of his own, and he had a vague sense of this world of his father's extending back to a time and a life before he himself was born. He was only a part of his father's world whereas his father belonged to his, Joby's, world in its entirety. And things were far from well in his father's world.

He moved a few steps nearer and his father did not look at him.

'They're all up at home, wondering where you are.'

He was close enough now to see a tiny insect creeping over his father's shirt collar and then crossing the gap on to his neck. He waited for him to brush it away.

'Who's there?'

149

His father made a quick movement of his hand and the insect disappeared.

'Me mam, an' Auntie Daisy an' Uncle Ted an' all. Happen they'll have gone now, though.'

'What had they to say?'

'I didn't hear much. Me Uncle Ted was asking me mam if she wanted to fetch the police.'

His father moved his shoulders and didn't reply.

'Me mam said she wouldn't, though. They sent me out then. Do they want the bobby to look for you, Dad?'

His father muttered, 'I expect so.'

Joby went and sank down on the grass beside his father. He watched thick white froth float by on the smooth black surface of the water.

'I wish we had a nice clean river like they have at Ilkley.' he said; 'then we'd happen get some fish in it.' He had once been on a Sunday School trip to Ilkley. It had been a wonderful day out.

Again his father said nothing, but shifted his position, sitting up now and hugging his knees, another blade of grass twisting and twirling in his strong fingers.

'Me Auntie Daisy and our Mona were round last night, late on,' Joby said. 'Our Mona was cryin' and me auntie said she'd been clouting her. She sounded mad and me mam stood up to her and told her where she got off. I was supposed to be in bed but I went down for a drink and listened through the door. Me mam didn't cry then but I think she did when they'd gone. I couldn't really tell 'cause she was sitting in the dark and she wouldn't let me put the light on ... Have you been away somewhere with our Mona?'

'You wouldn't understand, Joby,' his father said. 'You're too young.'

'You like our Mona, don't you?' Joby said after a time. 'I knew you did when I saw you cuddling her that time at me Auntie Daisy's when you were doing the washing-up. I've never seen you cuddling me mam . . .'

'You don't see everything,' his father growled. 'You see a damn' sight too much as it is.'

Joby looked down at the grass between his legs. He was some time in deciding to ask the next question because it was something which had never occurred to him before and could hardly have entered his mind before he experienced the sight of his father sitting alone on the river bank in his best clothes; not his father but a man, sitting alone with his world pulled about him like a cloak.

'D'you like our Mona better than me mam?' he said finally. 'Did you go away so's you could be with her?'

His father uttered a groan and put his face down on his knees.

'I've done summat I'll never live down . . . I'll never be able to look 'em all in the face again.' He was silent for a few moments, then he lifted his head. 'Why don't you hoppit an' leave me alone? What did you want to come down here for in t'first place, anyway?'

'I was just wandering about,' Joby said. 'They made me go out so's they could talk an' I didn't know where to go so I came down here.'

'You should be at home in bed, out of it all. It's got nowt to do with you. What d'you want to come getting mixed up in it for?'

151

Darkness was gathering about the tree-tops of the wood beyond the fields on the far side of the river. The river itself took on a sinister aspect in the fading light.

'It's getting dark,' Joby said. 'Me mam'll be wondering where we are.'

'She'll be wondering where *you* are,' his father said. 'You'd better be getting off home.'

'D'you want me to tell her I've seen you?'

'I reckon you won't be able to help yourself.'

Joby stood up reluctantly. It was a fair way home and it would take him a longer time to walk back because of his sore heel.

'Aren't you coming?'

'Not just yet. I'll sit here a while longer.'

'Have I to tell her you're coming?' Joby said.

His father hugged his knees in the dusk. 'Tell her what you like . . . Go on, get off. It's turning chilly and you've nowt much on you. You'll catch cold.'

Joby walked away from him. He crossed the path and went up a slope and through a gap in the hawthorn hedge of the meadow. He paused then and glanced back at his father before setting out to cut diagonally across the field. When he had gone a short way he stopped and looked back again but although the meadow was several feet above the river bank the line of the hedge barred his view. He felt a fiery twinge of pain in his heel at every step. He thought that the skin must be broken now and he didn't see how he would manage to walk home in the shoe.

He examined the ground for cow pats then sat down and gently eased the shoe off his foot. His sock was stuck to his heel and he gingerly pulled it off and peered at the inflamed skin. No, it wasn't broken yet, but it soon would be. He had nothing to pad it with, either. If he used his hanky he wouldn't get his shoe on. And anyway, he hadn't a hanky with him. Perhaps if he didn't tie the laces and walked very slowly, putting that foot down with great care . . . He put his sock on and then the shoe. He stood up with the shoe unfastened but made no move to go. He found himself looking back towards the river and wondering what his father was doing. There came vividly into his mind then the picture of the solitary figure in best clothes sitting beside the black water. And then he was thinking of the river being dragged for a woman who had disappeared. And Snap's uncle.

A moment later he was running back the way he had come, the stumbling impact of his feet on the tussocky grass stabbing a red-hot knife into his heel so that he felt the sweat starting on his forehead and he clamped his lips together to stop himself from crying out.

His father was not where he had left him. He looked both ways along the riverside in the dusk and there was no sign of him at all. Nothing except the flattened patch of grass where he had been sitting.

Joby said 'Dad' in a soft tremulous voice and went as far down the bank as he dared to look at the water. A faint rank odour rose from it and touched his nostrils. He turned away, his heart fluttering wildly. 'What can I do?' he said out loud. 'Oh, what can I do?'

He lifted his head and shouted, 'Dad! Dad! Where are you?'

He sensed rather than saw the movement behind a

clump of elder bushes before his father stepped into view, his hands adjusting his trousers. Joby hurled himself at him and clutched him round the waist.

'Oh, Dad, I was scared. I came back to look for you and you weren't there.' He hung on to his father, sobbing openly with relief.

'I thought I told you to go home?'

'I couldn't go without you. I was scared of leaving you down here by yourself. Oh, come on home with me, Dad. It'll be all right. Me mam's waiting for you. You don't care about me Auntie Daisy an' them, do you? They don't matter to us, do they?'

Weston touched his son's head. 'No, I don't reckon they do when it comes right down to it.' He pushed Joby gently away from him. 'Come on, then, stop your roarin'. You don't want your mam to see you like that, do you?' He fished the big handkerchief from his hip pocket and pushed it into Joby's hand.

'Here, use that.'

In a moment they were walking together towards the gap in the hedge and Weston became aware of Joby's difficulty.

'Is there summat wrong with your foot?'

'Me shoe's rubbing it. It's ever so sore.'

'Think you can manage to walk home?'

'I don't think I can. I think it'll start bleeding in a minute.'

'Hold on.' Weston squatted in a collier's crouch in the middle of the path. 'Get up on me shoulders an' I'll see'f I can carry you.'

Joby got up with his thighs on each side of his father's neck and Weston rose to his full height. He

154

began to walk with long steady strides while Joby swayed gently from side to side above him.

'All right?' Weston said.

'All right if you are,' Joby said.

'Is'll manage. You've got to be a bit heavier since I last carried you like this.'

There was nowhere for Joby to hold on to with his hands, but his father's hands were gripped firmly round his legs, just below his knees, and after a little way he had got the hang of balancing and swaying to the motion of his father's strides. He sensed his father relapsing into thought and he curbed his own desire to chatter. There was, after all, nothing much to say now. He rode in silence, looking about him at the approaching night. He was eight feet tall and from where he rode he could see the lights of the town sprinkled all over the dark hillside. Somewhere among them was the light of home. He couldn't see it, but he knew it was there.

1st May 65

TITLES IN THE NEW WINDMILL SERIES

Chinua Achebe: *Things Fall Apart*
Louisa M. Alcott: *Little Women*
Elizabeth Allen: *Deitz and Denny*
Eric Allen: *The Latchkey Children*
Margery Allingham: *The Tiger in the Smoke*
Michael Anthony: *The Year in San Fernando*
Bernard Ashley: *A Kind of Wild Justice*
Enid Bagnold: *National Velvet*
Martin Ballard: *Dockie*
Stan Barstow: *Joby*
H. Mortimer Batten: *The Singing Forest*
Nina Bawden: *On the Run; The Witch's Daughter; A Handful of Thieves; Carrie's War;
   Rebel on a Rock; The Robbers*
Rex Benedict: *Last Stand at Goodbye Gulch*
Phyllis Bentley: *The Adventures of Tom Leigh*
Paul Berna: *Flood Warning*
Judy Blume: *It's Not the End of the World*
Pierre Boulle: *The Bridge on the River Kwai*
E. R. Braithwaite: *To Sir, With Love*
D. K. Broster: *The Gleam in the North*
F. Hodgson Burnett: *The Secret Garden*
Helen Bush: *Mary Anning's Treasures*
Betsy Byars: *The Midnight Fox*
A. Calder-Marshall: *The Man from Devil's Island*
John Caldwell: *Desperate Voyage*
Ian Cameron: *The Island at the Top of the World*
Albert Camus: *The Outsider*
Victor Canning: *The Runaways; Flight of the Grey Goose*
Charles Chaplin: *My Early Years*
Erskine Childers: *The Riddle of the Sands*
John Christopher: *The Guardians; The Lotus Caves; Empty World*
Richard Church: *The Cave; Over the Bridge; The White Doe*
Colette: *My Mother's House*
Alexander Cordell: *The Traitor Within*
Margaret Craven: *I Heard the Owl Call my Name*
Roald Dahl: *Danny, Champion of the World; The Wonderful Story of Henry Sugar;
   George's Marvellous Medicine*
Andrew Davies: *Conrad's War*
Meindert deJong: *The Wheel on the School*
Peter Dickinson: *The Gift; Annerton Pit*
Eleanor Doorly: *The Radium Woman; The Microbe Man; The Insect Man*
Gerald Durrell: *Three Singles to Adventure; The Drunken Forest; Encounters with Animals*
Elizabeth Enright: *The Saturdays*
J. M. Faulkner: *Moonfleet*
C. S. Forester: *The General*
Jane Gardan: *The Hollow Land*
Eve Garnett: *The Family from One End Street; Further Adventures of the Family from One End
   Street*
G. M. Glaskin: *A Waltz through the Hills*
Rumer Godden: *Black Narcissus*
Kenneth Graham: *Wind in the Willows*
Graham Greene: *The Third Man* and *The Fallen Idol*
Grey Owl: *Sajo and her Beaver People*
John Griffin: *Skulker Wheat and Other Stories*
G. and W. Grossmith: *The Diary of a Nobody*
René Guillot: *Kpo the Leopard*
Jan De Hartog: *The Lost Sea*

Erik Haugaard: *The Little Fishes*
Esther Hautzig: *The Endless Steppe*
Bessie Head: *When Rain Clouds Gather*
Ernest Hemingway: *The Old Man and the Sea*
John Hersey: *A Single Pebble*
Nigel Hinton: *Getting Free; Buddy*
Alfred Hitchcock: *Sinister Spies*
C. Walter Hodges: *The Overland Launch*
Geoffrey Household: *Rogue Male; A Rough Shoot; Prisoner of the Indies; Escape into Daylight*
Fred Hoyle: *The Black Cloud*
Irene Hunt: *Across Five Aprils*
Henry James: *Washington Square*
Josephine Kamm: *Young Mother; Out of Step; Where Do We Go From Here?; The Starting Point*
Erich Kästner: *Emil and the Detectives; Lottie and Lisa*
M. E. Kerr: *Dinky Hocker Shoots Smack!; Gentlehands*
Clive King: *Me and My Million*
John Knowles: *A Separate Peace*
Marghanita Laski: *Little Boy Lost*
D. H. Lawrence: *Sea and Sardinia; The Fox* and *The Virgin and the Gypsy; Selected Tales*
Harper Lee: *To Kill a Mockingbird*
Laurie Lee: *As I Walked Out One Mid-Summer Morning*
Ursula Le Guin: *A Wizard of Earthsea; The Tombs of Atuan; The Farthest Shore; A Very Long Way from Anywhere Else*
Doris Lessing: *The Grass is Singing*
C. Day Lewis: *The Otterbury Incident*
Lorna Lewis: *Leonardo the Inventor*
Martin Lindsay: *The Epic of Captain Scott*
David Line: *Run for Your Life; Mike and Me; Under Plum Lake*
Kathleen Lines: *The House of the Nightmare; The Haunted and the Haunters*
Joan Lingard: *Across the Barricades; Into Exile; The Clearance; The File on Fräuline Berg*
Penelope Lively: *The Ghost of Thomas Kempe*
Jack London: *The Call of the Wild; White Fang*
Carson McCullers: *The Member of the Wedding*
Lee McGiffen: *On the Trail to Sacramento*
Wolf Mankowitz: *A Kid for Two Farthings*
Olivia Manning: *The Play Room*
Jan Mark: *Thunder and Lightnings; Under the Autumn Garden*
James Vance Marshall: *A River Ran Out of Eden; Walkabout; My Boy John that Went to Sea; A Walk to the Hills of the Dreamtime*
David Martin: *The Cabby's Daughter*
J. P. Martin: *Uncle*
John Masefield: *The Bird of Dawning; The Midnight Folk; The Box of Delights*
W. Somerset Maugham: *The Kite and Other Stories*
Guy de Maupassant: *Prisoners of War and Other Stories*
Laurence Meynell: *Builder and Dreamer*
Yvonne Mitchell: *Cathy Away*
Honoré Morrow: *The Splendid Journey*
Bill Naughton: *The Goalkeeper's Revenge; A Dog Called Nelson; My Pal Spadger*
E. Nesbit: *The Railway Children; The Story of the Treasure Seekers*
E. Neville: *It's Like this, Cat*
Wilfrid Noyce: *South Col*
Robert C. O'Brien: *Mrs Frisby and the Rats of NIMH; Z for Zachariah*
Scott O'Dell: *Island of the Blue Dolphins*
George Orwell: *Animal Farm*
Katherine Paterson: *Jacob Have I Loved*